Dedalus Retro
Mr Narrator

Pat Gray was born in Belfast. Between 1979 and 1981 he lived and worked in Morocco as a teacher. Since then he has worked extensively in Eastern Europe, but now lives in London.

He is the author of five novels: *Mr Narrator* (1989/2023), *The Political Map of the Heart* (2001), *The Cat* (1997/2015), *Dirty Old Tricks* (2020) and *The Redemption Cut* (2022).

PAT GRAY

MR NARRATOR

Dedalus

Supported using public funding by
**ARTS COUNCIL
ENGLAND**

Published in the UK by Dedalus Limited
24-26, St Judith's Lane, Sawtry, Cambs, PE28 5XE
email: info@dedalusbooks.com
www.dedalusbooks.com

ISBN printed book 978 1 915568 02 1
ISBN ebook 978 1 915568 03 8

Dedalus is distributed in the USA & Canada by SCB Distributors
15608 South New Century Drive, Gardena, CA 90248
email: info@scbdistributors.com www.scbdistributors.com

Dedalus is distributed in Australia by Peribo Pty Ltd
58, Beaumont Road, Mount Kuring-gai, N.S.W 2080
email: info@peribo.com.au www.peribo.com.au

First Published by Dedalus in 1989
Retro edition in 2023

Mr Narrator copyright © Pat Gray 1989/2023

The right of Pat Gray to be identified as the author of this work has been
asserted by him in accordance with the Copyright, Designs and Patents Act,
1988
Printed by Clays Ltd, Elcograf S.p.A.
Typeset by City Printers

A CIP Catalogue record for this book is available from the British Library

TUESDAY 31ST SEPTEMBER

Another odd letter from Société Herzog this morning, dated 12th September, and postmarked Beni Driss. I can't work out how it came to be posted from there, since Beni Driss, as far as I know, is nothing more than a waterstop on the main bus route up to Zef from the capital. It is signed by Munton, the head of the *service de comptabilité*. Try as I may I cannot see him posting anything from there, as it is certainly not his kind of place: it has no trunk dialling, no women, no French coffee, and the fine dust would annoy him, sticking to his one pair of highly polished brown shoes. The heat would bring his neck up in a rash under the soiled white collar.

The letter is short, written hurriedly, the writing unsteady as if composed in the back of a speeding taxi.

'I am most unhappy about this pump–house deal of yours, and we seem to have got really bogged down at the Ministry of Economic Affairs. There's some bastard called Zoboti whose been at us all week on the designs, though I'm none too sure who he is, or how he even came to hear about it. Mechti believes clearance will be difficult "*at the present time*", and a certain amount of the usual oiling will be necessary.' There follows some other routine business, neatly typed on a separate sheet, and a reference to some girl in the capital, who had impressed Munton by her "lizard-like qualities". He has always intrigued me with his choice of metaphors.

Anyway, the letter is here, on the Société Herzog's headed paper, heavily embossed, with the names of the directors crawling in Arabic all over the heading. The crest is a steam-ship of the old type, with a large red 'H' on its yellow funnel. Things are always difficult, especially clearances, though it is unusual for anything to impress Munton enough to require underlining. There is (as far as I am aware) nothing peculiar about the present time to warrant an underlining. Maybe there has been an event at the ministry, some re-shuffle, some re-alignment of forces, perhaps a half-hearted purge of sorts, which has unseated Munton's usual contacts, leaving the whole business suspended. As for Zoboti, I have no clear idea who he might be. He swims in my consciousness, below the level of reason, faintly threatening, like the first stirrings of an early morning nightmare. His first manifestation is as one of those extraordinarily large Arabs, one who rises to greet me from a wicker chair outside the Café de France. He has a jowly, expressionless face, and a handshake with the palm dry, the muscles of the fingers firm and impossible to avoid. He is the end of business. He blocks out the sun. In fact, if I do have to meet Zoboti, as I am sure I will, I would much rather have a man of the second type; a fumbled tap on the shoulder in some Sky View Lounge of some international hotel, and a figure on patent shoes with a copy of *Glamour Girls* concealed in the jacket pocket and a digital watch beeping uncontrollably on the wrist. The conversation would be easier, and once the necessary repartee was established, his motives for refusing to approve our plans could be exposed as unfounded. Concessions would be made. Another drink in the Sky View Lounge might be enough, a reminder that he, Zoboti, was at the head of the pack, part of the 20th century, a success.

These two Zobotis are the opposite poles of the possibilities implied in Munton's note to me. The underoccupied mind endlessly gives form to one's anxieties and an ill-defined gloom settles on me, the smell of an expensive lounge bar the morning after, as I file the letter with the others, the notes and documents celebrating the marriage in trade of Africa and Europe.

Later, in the evening of the same day, I was interrupted by Murphy, who has the other room. I could hear him coming, the noise of the keys in the security doors below echoing in the stairwell, then the steps, shuffling slightly, and the pause, to light a cigarette. At the summit, at the entrance to the flat, he pulled out another key and apparently dropped a handful of loose change down through the bannisters, because I could hear him swearing, and the tinkling of the money as it fell.

The outside door opened. He was talking to someone. I could hear a girl's voice, speaking in French.

'*Non, je ne veux pas . . . qu'est-ce qu'il va penser . . .*' and Murphy, overbearing in his terrible French, arguing back. My door opened and Murphy came in, went out, tried to pull the girl in with him. I could see on her wrist where he had seized it, a gold bracelet.

'*Ecoute* . . ., said Murphy to the girl, '*Ecoute, il va penser rien . . .*' and pulled her in, holding her in front of me. The girl was very beautiful, though she held her face away from me, from us both, still struggling.

'Meet Maria,' said Murphy.

'Bonjour Maria,' I said.

'Bonjour M'sieur,' she mumbled, broke free from his grip, and slid out through the door. Murphy raised his eyes to the heavens.

'Great little girl,' he said.

'Will she be all right out there?'

'Oh, Maria? Yes she'll be fine. A great girl. A bit shy, that's all.'

'Where d'you find her?'

'Now that'd be telling.'

He grinned, swaying slightly from side to side. His hands gripped the edge of my table. The freckles (the women here find them magnetic) and his eyes behind the pebble spectacles were charismatic in a disturbing way. Then he reached inside his jacket and pulled out a small bundle of papers.

'I'd like you to read this, Narrator,' he said. Various other items were unleashed along with those he intended me to read. Some complex illustrated instructions for the use of an experimental contraceptive device, a letter from a cosmologist in Aberdeen, a note from a girl, perhaps the girl he had brought, '*Tu es la lune et le ciel . . .*' For days later, I kept finding these items from Murphy's pockets amongst my documents.

However, the purpose of his visit to me, in addition to any other purpose he might have had, was to reveal his latest work. Murphy is a writer and his works come into my hands at various times during my stay here, through various means, depending on the state of our relationship. There are long periods when there is nothing, either because nothing is being produced, or because Murphy is engaged in 'honing up', 'cutting out', or 'sorting down' something which I have already seen. At other times he will become defensive, secreting pages of script clumsily when I enter the room where he is working. There is a surprising insecurity in much that he does. The text he offered me today gives a fair idea of his style:

' "Fuck, it's hot!"

The day was hot. The buildings were white, almost gleaming. McGuire looked at the clock.

"Not as hot as yesterday."

The girl smiled secretly. Her thin hand ran around the edge of her coffee cup. A faint whistling noise.

"It certainly is hot."

Steam rose from the pavement. The thin waiter was hosing the tiles again. He looked away. Nothing.

The girl picked at the crumbs of her last croissant, rearranging them. Patterns.

"Maybe we could . . ., began McGuire.

"Yes?" said the girl, picking her nose.

"Maybe we could . . ." He stopped and looked at her.

A stork flapped over the street.

"I don't think so," she said, before he could finish.'

As I read, he hovered anxiously, his hands idly fondling various items on my desk. I told him I liked it. He nodded, and said 'Uhuh?' He looked ill. His hands played with my alarm clock. Then he managed to set the bell ringing and dropped it on the table in surprise, from where it vibrated across a pile of receipts, and crashed to the floor. His hands worked too slowly. He picked the clock up, fumbling various dislodged pieces back together.

'Jesus, I'm sorry Narrator. Look, I'm genuinely sorry.'

'It's OK. Its just a clock.'

'Shit,' he said. Then added 'could you just read it, y'know tell me what you think?'

Then he left the room, suddenly restless, perhaps fearing criticism.

'*Tu as fini?*' I heard the girl's voice, right outside my door, as if her ear had been pressed against it.'*Il est Anglais, ton ami?*' she asked. Then the door of Murphy's room closed, and I returned to his text.

'He was silent for some time. Another stork crossed over the street and settled on its nest. The Catholic Church. His hands lay idle. The newspaper lay unread. The girl breathed quietly and thought about lunch.

"Let's fuck," said McGuire.

"What?"

"Let's fuck."

The clock struck uncertainly, scaring the storks.

"I'd like another coffee," said the girl.

"OK," said McGuire, snapping his fingers at the empty morning cafe.'

This was a bad sign. I went to bed, with the two Zobotis still there, balanced on the scales of tomorrow's possibilities.

WEDNESDAY 1ST OCTOBER.
THE MORNING.

I began the day with an attempt to unravel the meaning behind Munton's letter. Who exactly was Zoboti? Where had he emanated from? Why was he interfering with my pump-house? What possible interest could he have in something so essentially uninteresting? Of course, other things hung on it. If you like, the pump–house was pretty well central to a whole strategy of idleness, and if the pump–house got the bureaucratic turn-down then the trunnel joints would get it too. It was therefore with a sense of urgency that I called in on Bicycle Repair Man, not because I had a bicycle to repair but because Repair Man had a cousin who worked at the Ministry of Economic Affairs in the capital, and I had a friendship with him based on some chance events unlikely enough to give us both cause to smile each time we met. The most unexpected people have relatives in unexpectedly high positions, though just how high it is often difficult to judge.

Repair Man inhabited (during daylight hours) a shack at the end of my road, just at that fortunate point where the tarmac petered out, on a corner which the students at the New University cycled past on their way to lectures or demonstrations. As a result, his trade was good, and his shack showed the consequences of each new expansion in learning. When the faculty of law had opened, a new extension had been built, in corrugated perspex. His shop was always encircled by people, as it was an excellent point from which to observe — or prey upon — the passing traffic which converged there from different sections of the town. As I approached, I could hear the bony rattle of dice, the murmurings of gossip, the sounds of mechanical work, the babble of voices. Inside sat Repair Man, at the heart of an invisible but still perceptible web. Above him hung a picture of his cousin in a Chinese plastic frame, and above that another picture, of the King, cyclostyled, in full tribal regalia. The picture of the

6

cousin was a symbol of influence, a reminder to all who entered Repair Man's door that their words would not be ignored in the capital, while that of the King assured the authorities of Repair Man's loyalty, on the surface of things at least. Below the picture of the cousin was an illustrated certificate from the course Repair Man had attended in Zef, in the summer of 1937, under the auspices of the Peugeot company. At the very bottom of the planked rear wall was a collection of genuine unused Peugeot inner tubes for bicycles. The combination of all these factors made Repair Man a figure of some influence in the community.

As I entered he stood ponderously to greet me, with the special smile reserved for his acquaintances who could afford to travel by train frequently.

'Aaah, M. Narrator, what a great pleasure. Will you have some tea? How is your business? How is the madman Murphy? Everything is progressing?' He pulled out a chair from under a brother who was playing patience in the corner of the shack, kicked the legs straight, wiped it with an oily rag, and I sat down. The brother collected his playing cards and moved outside onto the pavement and into the sunlight, where he squatted and resumed his interrupted game. I told him Murphy was writing again, that business prospered, the world turned. He beamed at me, encouragingly, pouring green tea from a slender pot, holding it high so the liquid frothed and bubbled in the glass. We exchanged pleasantries, until at length he said:

'Why do we have the honour of this visit? I see that your mind is not fixed on the usual regularities.' I nodded, and he turned to check that the card player was beyond earshot. His face became less affable, greyer in the poor light. It was a pliable face, curiously rubberised, flexible to respond to the calculating emotionality which he saw to be a necessity in business. The strain of this had carved tiny wrinkles in unexpected directions across the skin. It was a foreign face, not unattractive, but written upon by experiences a European maybe could not share. As the conversation became serious, and as I explained the sudden obstructions which had emerged to my business, an air of professionalism, almost like that of a family doctor, came upon him, listening and yet not listening, as if his mind were also hearing the requests of others, from earlier in the day, the week, the month, relayed to him simultaneously with my own enquiries. Outside, I could hear the sound of a bicycle tyre being inflated. By now he had established himself firmly on an empty crate, having wiggled his buttocks energetically to assure the necessary comfort for a truly sympathetic listening pose.

'You think there is trouble in the capital?' he asked.

'Well, I think there may be.'

'It's a difficult business.'

'What is?'

'The capital. Problems at the political level. You know it is all-pervasive.'

'But what particularly? Do you know who Zoboti is?'

'Ah, Monsieur, you are aware that my knowledge of politics is unnaturally limited.'

Bicycle Repair Man glanced at the portrait of his cousin, hanging there in the gloom, as if establishing some link, telepathically, with the Ministry of Economic Affairs.

'Your cousin? He has said nothing?' I asked. He smiled, faintly bemused, a slight tremor in the pause before he spoke.

'When he speaks, I do not necessarily listen.'

'But I thought you held him in the highest regard.'

'Did hold. I did hold him in the highest regard, but of course now I see him for what he is. He is a *buvard*, a bluebottle on the camel's backside, he is the dregs of the bottle of life!'

His features worked to form themselves into the necessary look of contempt. The torrent of abuse gathered strength.

'He is not a man. I was mistaken in this. He is a *gamin* amongst men! It grieves me to think that he is of the same family.'

In the end, his insults began to lose their force, the words became slower, the tongue searched tiredly for new metaphors, and then came a silence, interrupted briefly by the sound of two draughts players arguing outside in the sun. His face sagged, became suddenly morose. Something had indeed happened in the capital, necessitating the breaking of the bonds of family, admiration, and influence.

'Have you heard anything from him?' He looked around now, as if the mentioning of the cousin again would bring further ill–defined misfortunes down upon him.

'Nothing.'

'He hasn't written?'

'Not in three months.' There was a pause. He clasped and unclasped his big hands, the fingernails dirty and cracked. A heavy lorry rumbled past outside in low gear. His lips moved, but it was not clear if he had spoken or not. The noise of the lorry faded like some passing apocalypse.

'I am sorry. I am not myself, it is you I should be helping. I promise everyone everything. I promise my brother a free travel warrant to Rigadir. The deputy chief wanted his Mercedes cleared by the Douane. I gave them my word, but since my cousin is gone, who knows? The wheels they do not turn without greasing, you know, and my cousin, well, he was in a unique position, exceptionally well placed. Currency permits, he had access to currency permits. Can you imagine where one must be to get such things?'

'Do you know where he has gone?'

'Nothing. I do not know. I am ruined. It is ruination here not to keep faith. I can hear them laughing already. Every time I hear merriment, I imagine it is at my own downfall.'

'But is your cousin all right?'

'I don't know. Every time I think of him, I think of my own ruin. I promised the wife of the director of the cement works a passport for her sister. As for where he might be, well that is another problem. Mohammed went to the capital last week, travelled up in the big Berliet to the very gates of the Ministry, but they wouldn't even let him in through the door. At one point they attempted to arrest him for aggravated loitering, and in the end it all got him down so much that he swapped his return ticket for some cheap woman, and had to come back by bus. Everything about this affair is terrible. Now you say there is some Zoboti who has taken

9

over! I have a bad feeling on this. I think there will be more trouble. I put people off you know? I put them off by saying my cousin is busy on important projects, planning an electric pumping system for the vineyards, but excuses come to an end, there is not a great deal of repetition in them.'

'He cannot just vanish,' I said, more to raise his spirits than for anything else.

'Can't he?' Repair Man fumbled vaguely amongst the folds of his djellaba, emerging finally with a greasy but once official looking slip of paper. The sight of it seemed to disturb him, as if it gave off a harmful light, because he averted his eyes, only to have them rest for a moment on the photograph of the cousin, there behind the glass, smiling. He thrust the paper at me, refusing to look at it. It was in the last stages of disintegration, and had, at some stage, been crumpled and uncrumpled several times. It was a tax demand.

'You see,' he said. 'It cannot be an error. It is something systematic. Errors one can suffer, because they do not continue in the same path, they have no ultimate purpose. This, however, this proves that there is a purpose in what they are doing. Only a man disgraced, or the relative of one, receives a tax demand. A tax demand is a sure sign that one is no longer as consequential as one thought.'

His head sagged lower. I noticed for the first time a bald patch, with an ugly scar running across it, jagged at the edges; as if a zip opened into his brain.

'Have you seen anyone about this?' I asked.

'There is no point. Stupidity cannot be evaded, it follows along inexorably, like a limping dog, never giving up. The cleverer you are the less easy it is to escape, because the less you can imagine the kind of stupidity that gives rise to these kind of acts, and hence you cannot even begin to predict what will happen next.'

His head nodded from side to side loosely, as if in conversation with himself, a hidden mechanism of self-justification whispering restoring phrases.

'Look at that,' he said suddenly, pointing to a small photo that stood beside the spirit stove he used for brewing tea. The

10

photo showed him astride a large motorcycle, squat, black, and with a big old–fashioned headlight.

'That day I went from here to Jerada in eight minutes.'

Behind him in the photo stood his entire family, holding various trophies: a casette recorder, certificates, a musket. The photo was yellow, curled at the edges, the figures vague and ghostly, caught in a fading moment of success.

'Maybe it is all a mistake.'

'Tax demands are not mistakes.'

I felt drawn in, sucked down, and found myself somehow wishing for a revival of his initial affability.

'You must not let them see you like this,' I said.

'Keep up the good face?'

'You must keep it up, yes. Maybe there is something that I can do?' He looked up, seized the words with his hands as they floated through the air.

'My friend, if only you could!' He said, an arm around my shoulders. 'We could ... I could see to it that you got ...' Then, remembering how little he had to offer he stopped. There was a silence for a moment.

'If you could make it soon, very soon Monsieur. There are matters of the greatest urgency. If you, with your friends, your other contacts, you know with Europeans things are frequently different.' He was interrupted by a gentle insistent tapping on the door.

'Ahmed, the wife of the director is here,' said the voice of the brother outside. Repair Man's smile came through weakly. He opened the door.

'Madame, what a great pleasure it is to see you.' He chivied away two boys who were betting on a draughts game on the pavement.

'You know I deplore all forms of gambling,' he cried, squeezing my shoulder as he guided me out, to remind me of our agreement.

It was only when I was outside that I realised I had no clear notion of how I could assist him without implicating myself in his decline. Still later, as the taxi I hailed swept me away, I wondered if I should even try. The taxi wandered epileptically down Boulevard de Nada, eventually dropping me before the newstand on Rue Mujdib, where I resumed my quest for information on the capital by buying a copy of *Le Matin du Sahara,* a flabby, featureless paper, like uncooked pastry to the touch. Only at moments of grave crisis would reference be made in it to real and important events, when a point was reached where everyone in the country could not fail to notice that something was amiss, and to refuse to acknowledge it could only be attributed to total blindness on the part of the government, rather than the merely partial blindness to which the people were accustomed.

Today, the paper lay limp and uninspiring in my hands, as I lounged under the pineapple plant in the Cafe Rubric. There appeared to be no exciting news at all. The lead story concerned the conference of co-operative orange growers in Gouger, and consisted mainly of lists of figures for orange production. There was an underexposed photograph of a man's face, dominated by teeth and a pair of curious spectacles. He was reading from a text, and the caption was immensely long: '*Monsieur Boujloud, le nouveau secretaire général de la société coopérative des commerçants d'oranges délivrant son discours à l'occasion de la vingt-neuvième conférence à Gouger.*' I found myself thinking of Repair Man again. Somehow, he had worked on my conscience absurdly. I could not concentrate on the newspaper. Boujloud swam in front of my unfocused eyes, his spectacles like goggles. Maybe they were part of the orange grower's equipment, and the new secretary general was making some obscure populist statement? A stork flapped its way over the street, the creaking of its wings suddenly audible during a pause in the passing traffic.

On the inside pages, the King was again meeting a delegation from Upper Volta. There were details of a new scheme to develop irrigation in the mountains, and a picture of another serious man reading from a paper. In fact he looked suspiciously like Monsieur Boujloud from the front page, even down to the curious spectacles. '*Monsieur Zoboti, a l'occasion de …*' began the caption, then degenerated into an impressively smudged misprint the shape of a salamander. I looked carefully at the misprint, but could discern no meaning in it. The man, however, was Zoboti, and it is by no means a common name. Maybe, to be more correct, he was *a* Zoboti, rather than the particular one I was looking for. Naturally there was always an outside chance that he was the actual individual, the one who had stamped *annulé* in big red letters across the Société Herzog's request for import clearance, and sent Repair Man's cousin from his swivel chair in the Ministry of Economic Affairs. In the photo he addressed the crowd, his mouth like a dash in a hurriedly typed and angry text. He was spitting out some word at the end of a sentence, probably '*interdit*' or '*absolument interdit*'. It was diffi-cult to tell behind the goggles, with thick tinted lenses, as the eyes were invisible, like sharks imagined below the surface of water. The rest of the face was fairly formless, a sort of admin-istrative face with substantial muscles under the pink flab, muscles to clamp down on words and draw in gulps of air, so denunciations could be made without pausing for breath. He could well be the man. Not content with removing Repair Man's cousin, he had had sufficient energy to move against Repair Man's family, root and branch. Maybe the Monsieur Boujloud was a cousin of Zoboti's, and a new appointee? They both looked the kind of men who would launch new and dangerous initiatives after lunch, with only a cursory consideration of consequences. I examined the damaged caption again, and the photo. On the lapel there was some kind of mark — a curious shape — perhaps an enamel badge of some sort, resembling nothing so much as a parrot or macaw.

I clapped my hands for the waiter.

'Ahmed, could you get me another copy of *Le Matin*?'

'But Monsieur, you have one already.'

'I know, but the print is damaged on this one.'

'That is extraordinary! Why not give it to me and I will exchange it!'

'Well, I'd rather not. There are things still to be studied.'

'But if it is badly printed, how can you study it? You will only damage your eyes trying to read it.'

'No. It's all right. Can you just fetch me another one?'

'As you say,' he replied, limping away in his carpet slippers, to return with a fresh copy of *Le Matin*.

'I hope the print is satisfactory,' he said as he handed it over. I flicked hurriedly to the inside page. No Zoboti. A large picture of a Berliet lorry full of youths waving the national flag, and a dog in the foreground. It was the same edition, but Zoboti had disappeared, been sucked away. I turned again to the original photo. '*Monsieur Zoboti à l'occasion de …*' What occasion was it? I scanned the crowd that listened there in the photograph, like a school assembly, struggling to look one way while thinking in another, quite different way. On the left, incredibly, was Munton. The thin nose, head held to the right so the blue vein would not be visible to the photographer, and that civilised face, the pointy shoes.

Then I glanced up to see a large Arab holding some small object out to me.

'Monsieur, you may borrow my magnifying glass if you wish. It may help you to find that which you are seeking.' He spoke classical Arabic beautifully.

'Is it a friend of yours?' he enquired, indicating the picture in the open paper, and seating himself in the vacant chair beside me. The smell of aftershave came up disconcertingly from beneath his turban. I explained my problem.

'Ahh, with this you will discover everything,' he said, unfolding a gleaming glass from a tortoiseshell holder with a silver rivet in it. The sunlight bounced around inside the lense. He handled the glass like a magician.

'Here, with your permission I will show you. It is some-times difficult to get the range correct.'

He took my newspaper and the only photo of Zoboti gently in his hands, and set to it with the magnifying glass with delicate precision. The face, the lapel, loomed up distorted in the frame, looking out at us for a brief moment. On the lapel was an enamel parrot, upside down. I held the magician's hand over the spot, but they were held rigid, as if bolted to some steel structure beneath his all-concealing djel-laba. The parrot browned, curled, flamed. The big Arab was smiling distantly, looking out into the street, in apparent reverie.

'Hey, Monsieur, you're burning the paper!' I cried.

Then the flames took hold, blazing up the page, through Munton, through Zoboti's audience, through the other trash in the newspaper. The Arab turned slowly and a look of real-isation came upon him, his face filling with an expression of exquisite embarrassment . He flung the paper away, and it described a sizzling parabola out over the flowerbeds and into the road beyond.

'Monsieur, how dreadful, what an awful accident! You must allow me to buy you another. Ahmed! Please, a paper for Monsieur. Really, this is terrible! May I get you a coffee?'

WEDNESDAY 1ST OCTOBER.
THE AFTERNOON

After the accident with the newspaper, events resumed a more predictable course: I had a minor scene with Murphy. I had returned home for lunch, and found him there in the kitchen with the girl. They were cooking something together, the marble work top strewn with aubergines, the girl whipping up eggs and Murphy whistling. As I entered, the girl turned her back on me, and began some careful slicing actions, secretively, as if denying to herself that she was actually there.

'Say hullo to Narrator, Maria,' said Murphy. She ignored him.

'C'mon. He's not going to do you any harm.' She snapped something at him, and continued slicing with her back to us both.

'Pretty shy,' said Murphy, and tossed the aubergines into the pan, where they sizzled angrily. The girl turned towards him, but with her face still turned away from me. She wore a thin silk shirt, her skin was very dark against the white cloth. She had a pair of gold slippers on her feet.

'*Va-t-en! Ton ami ne vas pas vouloir cuisiner avec moi*, your friend will not want to cook with me,' she said.

'You want to bet?' said Murphy, and winked sideways.

'Go and talk to him about your famous book.' She pushed him gently towards me.

'What does he know about literature?'

'About as much as you know about cooking, perhaps.'

'Well, they're much the same.'

'Art and life, much the same altogether.'

'Now that depends.'

'*Ça dépend*. Always depending on something, you Europeans. This depends on that. That depends on this. I would do that if I wasn't doing this. If I do that I won't be able to do the other. Always some kind of interminable calculus!' As she talked the girl became more agitated, shook her head up and down. Her long hair, blue black, fell over her eyes. Suddenly she stopped, and let out a small embarrassed laugh, as if conscious of a minor indiscretion.

'She talks like that,' said Murphy.

'Why don't you go and talk about your book,' said the girl.

'So, you think we equivocate too much,' I replied.

'Equivocate, manipulate, prevaricate, obfuscate and dilate.'

Her eyes were quite extraordinarily black, so that nothing could be discerned in them other than their blackness. She was looking at me now.

'Dilate?'

'Dilute more like,' said Murphy.

'You see how easily you are drawn into foolish conversations that lead nowhere. Your friend Murphy is a master. Master of the vacuum and the abyss, if that is something to boast about.'

'It certainly is,' said Murphy. The girl could not have been old, but somewhere had acquired an education of extraordinary intensity, that seemed to leave the atmosphere in the room strained, vaguely fearful. She stirred the aubergines around in the pan, her movements spiky, as if enraged by an all consuming impatience that had suddenly swept upon her along with her bizarre conversation. Murphy patted her behind, like a proprietor, and she giggled carefully.

'Now, we mustn't get too serious on a Wednesday afternoon. Let us change the subject. Let us return to the book, Narrator. What did you think? Did you like that bit about let's fuck? I mean its surprising, I admit, but surprise is the thing in literature, isn't it?' The girl listened carefully, apparently trying to understand the English.

'Well, it's certainly stimulating,' I said.

'What do you like about it? You can't just say its stimulating. I mean how about this. "The avocado sliced easily. The pip came out round and shiny." I mean its just got to be a great line. I suppose I could cut it back more, but . . . I mean d'you think it's cut back enough? What about the storks? Surely they're superfluous?'

'Superfluous, what is superfluous?' asked the girl.

'This is serious,' said Murphy, waving her into silence. She continued cooking with an angry determination not to be offended.

'I think the storks are OK. They are languid after all, and that's what you're after,' I said.

'Languid, huh.' He said, vaguely disappointed.

'Well, languid with an underlying tension,' I said, correcting myself.

'Yeah! That's it.' He brightened, then reached inside his jacket and pulled out a handwritten page, torn from an exercise book.

'There's more. I mean it's really coming on.' He began to read, dramatically, his head thrown back, the paper held up before his peering spectacles.

'He took the lettuce, stripped the outside leaves. There was regularity in the gesture. Some of the leaves were yellow at the edges. He threw them in the bin.

"Bad lettuce," he said.

"Oh yeah?" she said from the couch.

The girl had turned now, and stood with her back to the wall, leaning, looking at him. He stopped and looked around. I smiled at him.

'I mean of course there's work to be done. I mean there's more to it.' He started reading again, this time less theatrically.

'He started on the tomatoes.

"I wish it was spring," she said.

"Underripe, imagine that."

"Yeah," she said, knocking the magazines on the floor.'

He stopped again.

'I mean what I want to do is to cut and cut again. I mean to really cut it back until its just raw, you know, really raw, with none of this symbolism. I don't know, I really don't. I've tried cutting ...' His hands made large purposeful gestures.

'It gets lost. You know.' His hand movements became vaguer, less certain. The girl picked a plum from a bowl of fruit on the side and began eating slowly, watching him.

'They're not ripe,' she said, smiling.

'Fuck off,' said Murphy. She continued to smile at him.

'Its fairly well cut back as it is.'

'Not enough, I want to get right back down to basics.'

'What do you mean?'

'Something without morality. Something entirely without morality. A lot of slobs who hang around sticking their fingers up each others anatomies. Morality is just so the educated can have something to talk about at long dinner parties.'

'A world without morality doesn't seem too nice to me,' said the girl, interrupting again, as if sure of the exact moment.

'Look, Maria, morality doesn't interest me at all.'

'*C'est évident*,' she said simply. For a moment I had the impression he was going to hit her, that was what he wanted.

There was a silence.

'I want to get back to bare essentials without becoming flat. I want to connect in some way to our grandest inner boredoms. To describe boredom without oneself being boring, if you can imagine that.' He continued with difficulty. The girl was whistling silently between her teeth now and adding cumin to the stew.

'I think its OK,' I said.

'OK? It's rubbish. Why's everyone so polite? It's quite impossible. I'm just trying to connect with people.' When he said connect, the word ended with an odd Irish twang to it, the final 'e' becoming an 'a', as if the word had an entirely different meaning, personal to him alone.

'I mean it's all a wilderness if it doesn't connect. Its quite a problem. I mean you think its easy, but it's not, to get the sort of reaction, the sort of response one wants.'

'The characters seem a bit flat. . . .'

'But that's what I want. I want them that way, so the slightest clues really stick out, really dominate the landscape, become inescapable when normally they'd be hidden in a flood of useless words, can you see?'

The girl, still eating delicately, looked across and raised her eyes almost imperceptibly, as if to say 'what can you expect?'

She finished the plum and dropped the pip into the bin. There was something about the whole of her movements that was extraordinarily insolent.

'Listen Murphy, don't lose your temper. It is not that serious,' she said.

'Maybe,' said Murphy, and they began to serve out their lunch together.

I returned to my room. Murphy had dropped a copy of *Le Matin du Sahara* on my table. I could hear them both laughing now. In the newspaper was the Berliet lorry, but no photograph of Zoboti.

It was thus with a growing sense of frustration that I called on my friend Mustafa later that afternoon, in order to use his telephone, or to use his skills as a telephone user. Through years of experience he had learned the art of negotiating open lines to all parts of the country. He had a command of the exchanges that was unequalled in the town, and in fact made more from his telephoning than he ever did through the running of his hotel.

Today as usual, I came upon him sitting cross legged on the steps of the Hotel Oasis, reading a copy of *El Zif* intently, with his one good eye screwed up, scanning part of the front page. The whole paper was folded into one tiny square, almost a cube, which included only the article he was interested in, so as not to distract the one good eye. A black cigarette fumed from the corner of his mouth, the smoke drifting unnoticed across the other eye, which could cause him neither pleasure nor pain. There is nothing quite like the intensity of a one-eyed man reading a newspaper.

'Hullo Mustafa, a beautiful day,' I said.

He looked up, and jumped to his feet.

'Monsieur Narrator, what a very great pleasure. It is some time since we have met. Sit down, sit down. The steps are newly swept, and we can talk in comfort. The sun doesn't slip behind the cinema until four at least these days.'

Overhead, the hotel sign creaked rustily in a stray gust of wind off the main boulevard.

'How are you? How are your business affairs? Will you be with us much longer? And your friend, that crazy reactionary you live with? What is his name? Murphdog? Murphdaz? How is he? I saw him the other day down in Café de Belgique with the fat Jew who owns the garage. He was most busy, with all sorts of papers over the table.'

'Ah yes, he is still writing.'

'How marvellous it must be to be an educated man. There are so many things one can do. I cannot really think why a man of his calibre comes here. He could be anything: Judge, Avocat, Professeur. I often wonder precisely what he writes. I'm not sure I'd like it, I mean to have all one's thoughts written down. I mean, after all people can check up on you, they can look at the page and it'll all be down there in black and white, permanently. If you speak, and speak only, people quickly forget.'

I agreed with him that literacy was an extraordinary thing, and in turn asked him how his business affairs were prospering.

'Business is always good of course, though it is not entirely the season. One week there are Germans with Volkswagens and water purifiers going down into the desert, the next a party of Tunisians buying light switches and vacuum cleaners. There is always variety. Variety is a great essential, as I'm sure you'll agree. Even today I received a letter from that young English boy that was here that had all the trouble. Perhaps you could translate it for me? He doesn't send the money or the shirts with the Beatles on the front, but no doubt he has his problems too.' He handed me a letter, still in its envelope, postmarked Dewsbury. I translated for him:

'My Dear Mustafa,

I am now home after all my difficulties and thanks to your kind help and hospitality. I have no job just yet because my head is still confused and I'm afflicted by odd and disturbing thoughts, but not so badly as before. I cannot send you the money just yet, but when things are better I will see you right.

I've got the shirt you wanted, but its not exactly a Beatles shirt. Its got some kind of carnivorous bird on it. I have sent it on in a separate parcel.

Kind regards, Brian.'

'There, you see!' said Mustafa. 'The boy continues to have difficulties. You Europeans can be fully trusted to pay what you owe. Men of integrity, except maybe the odd few. But it is a terrible business with the drugs. I cannot imagine firstly why such a boy would come here, and secondly, why he should poison himself. In the end he went quite crazy, believing that we were all conspiring against him, that the maid was spraying poison on the floors, that I was beaming knowledge up through the plugholes. He would not open the door, and when I called the doctor he jumped off the balcony and out into the street below. Can you imagine the scene? We gave him a great piqûre and put him to sleep in the maid's room until someone from the consulate came to take him back. Your organisation is remarkable in many ways.'

The whole story was related in a matter of fact way, as if it were an everyday occurrence. The Oasis Hotel tended to attract travellers of a certain kind.

'An unpleasant affair,' I said.

'Indeed,' he agreed, and looked out ruminatively over the baked earth of the street to the Cinema Royale. *The Great Dictator* was playing for its fourth week, and already the colour was beginning to fade from the posters. At length we came to the purpose of my visit.

'I have to telephone the capital. There seem to have been some changes that are causing trouble to a deal of mine.'

'A deal?'

'Oh, the usual.'

'You know you're the sixth person today who wants to telephone the capital. Important men too. They know they can rely upon my discretion. I even had the owner of the Hotel Zef, sweaty with urgency, with some questions that he did not feel he could ask in his own office. Oh yes, they have all been here, anxious to get on.'

'So the lines are open?'

'Yes, but regrettably time is short. This morning I spent three hours crouched over the mouthpiece shouting into it. At one point I even had a line to Spain by accident. All this goes on my bill you know, and I am not a rich man. There is really no money in it at all. Do you see the state of my finger?' He held his index finger forward for inspection. A large purple blister bulged below the finger nail.

'In fact Monsieur, telephoning presents such difficulty that maybe it would be better to go to the capital yourself. If you are there on their doorstep, in the flesh, it is somehow different. In the old days of course it was better, because we did not know what was going on until long after it had ceased to be of any importance.'

'10 Dirhams,' I said, cutting into his speculations.

'30', he said.

'That's absurd. A month ago you did it for 5.'

'Ah, but that was a month ago. There is always inflation to take into account. You think I make easy money here? You think I enjoy giving up my afternoons to telephone? I am not a telephone exchange you know!'

'15, and that's my last offer.'

'No, I am a man of honour. I cannot accept such a low price. 25 and you may take it or leave it. It does not worry me.'

I rose to my feet slowly.

'25 is an extortionate price, I do not know where you get these figures from.'

'My father often charged 40. It is only because you are a good and reliable friend that I give you a good price now.'

I began to walk away towards the corner.

'*Au revoir*,' he called. 'Come and see me again soon.'

I turned the corner, at any moment expecting to be called back. The main boulevard was busy with late afternoon traffic, and I could feel the day slipping away, fading agonisingly, with nothing of the Zoboti affair settled. Schoolgirls in nylon pinafores were moving home in droves before the evening curfew, laughing at the boys and flirting. The price was quite excessive, and I could not go back; it would represent some concession, some symbolic retreat. Then, of course, when I had given up hope and was least expecting it, there came the gentle tug at the corner of my coat, from below. I looked down upon a small face, all large brown eyes, looking up with innocent respect.

'Please, Monsieur, will you come back? Mustafa says that 20 Dirhams will do fine.'

The boy took my hand in his small palm, and we padded back round to the hotel. He stepped daintily over the body of a dead dog, wrinkling his nose in distaste as the flies lifted off the corpse, and let me into the interior of the Oasis. The floor was tiled, in big broken slabs, with dirt lodged between them, the kind of slabs the French had brought with them and been unable to take away. I could hear Mustafa dialling already from his office. A big Berber woman was swabbing down the stairs, and the water flooded down the steps, the rythmic swish of the mop relaxing in the gloom of the entrance lobby.

The boy stopped outside Mustafa's office, bowed from the waist in a mock display of chivalry, and ushered me in.

The blinds were down, and Mustafa had taken the padlock off the phone, a cigarette hanging again from his lower lip. There was total concentration in his telephoning. One hand, be-ringed, gestured me to the old armchair opposite his desk, stuffed with yellowing copies of *Le Matin du Sahara*. He dialled regularly, monotonously, with his left hand. When he failed to connect, there was no anger; he merely replaced the receiver, sighed vaguely, lifted the receiver, dialled again, listened, sighed, and repeated the process over again.

On the wall was a hunting scene in which a huge stag loomed uncertainly through a patch of mildew, looking down on a great waterfall in which a girl was washing her blonde hair. A monkey played in the trees. The colours were some-how wrong, with an almost electric, unnatural brightness. In the middle of the waterfall, someone had hung the 1964 Société des Postes et Telecommunications calendar, sus-pended on a nail driven into the wall. The darker corners of the room seemed to fade into emptiness, and a hatstand could be discerned, one of its branching hooks broken off, on the margins of the darkness. The dialling continued, and Mustafa ignored me as he worked, until suddenly he stiffened, leant right forward over his desk, pressing the receiver to his ear. He began to shout:

'Hullo. Hullo. Rue Prig? I want a line to the capital. Yes, Mustafa at the Hotel Oasis. It is a call of the utmost importance!' Here he looked at me to see if I appreciated the effort he was making.

'Yes, yes, Abdesalom is well, indeed he is.'

There followed some routine conversation about mutual friends, Mustafa rolling his eyes and pulling faces as he sighed, laughed and smiled appropriately into the telephone.

'Strike? There was no strike this morning. I telephoned twelve times and there was no strike. Can you not go through Beni Drar?' A hint of desperation crept into his voice.

'Yes, yes, it is of the very greatest crucialness. I have here a man who is from the embassy of the British Republic. He is here in front of me, I can see him from where I am sitting. No, he is not with the police, he is a diplomat. It is an affair of the greatest urgency. That is not your affair. You will call back? You promise? We await the ring of the bell with impatience.'

He put the receiver down, wiped his forehead, then smiled largely.

'You see, they are frightened if you mention someone they have not heard of before. They don't know where you fit in. You could be anything. You could be part of a special mission, somebody important. And of course you are foreign, so his curiosity will be redoubled and he will do everything possible to connect the cables, just so that he can hear what you have to say. If he doesn't, he won't know, and will be left alone in his exchange with only his own speculations for company.'

'But Britain is a monarchy.'

'All the better, we monarchies must stick together.'

He rubbed his hands, as if he had just satisfactorily completed a complex piece of woodwork requiring much ingenuity, and was looking forward to the next stage of the assembly process. The telephone rang again, suddenly, raucously, and he snatched it up in mid-peal.

'Hullo. Yes. YES. Beni Drar? Look, I want a line to the city, and I want it quickly, immediately . . . what? . . . what?'

Then his tone changed.

'Aaah, good morning director. I am ringing on behalf of a Monsieur Narrator, personal envoy of the Queen of the Republic of England, who must have a line to the city by five. I find that quite incredible. Put me through via Sidi Bouarfa, if that can be accomplished. Yes. Goughly . . . no, I don't know what the Queen's envoy is doing here. Yes, yes . . . he has a briefcase . . . thank you, I am most grateful.' He did not replace the receiver, but cradled it under his ear, pushing forward a pad of green paper and a pen.

'The NUMBER,' he whispered, and I hurriedly scrawled out Munton's office number at Société Herzog. The clock over the desk ticked towards the hour at which Munton would be slipping on his jacket, checking his supply of prophylactics, and making for his favourite steam bath. From the earpiece came a series of random clickings, fragments of overheard conversation, the murmurings of automatic relays on manual override. Mustafa suddenly cried out:

'Monsieur! Monsieur! The NUMBER . . . it rings,' and then his look of astonished pride began to disintegrate. I could faintly hear the burring of the phone at the other end, unanswered. I signalled to him to keep listening, but the sibilant burring continued. He slumped in his seat and fiddled with a packet of pills on the desk top. He flicked through some old correspondence, made a brief note on the edge of a letter, picked his nose.

'I'm sorry, Mustafa, they must be out. Sometimes in the office, you know, the secretaries gossip, they paint their nails. Its most difficult.'

He replaced the receiver, and the link with the capital was cut.

'Ah, Monsieur, is it not what I have been saying? Communication. As through a darkling glass. Am I right?'

He leant back and said 'Ten Dirhams', as if to terminate any further speculation. I unfurled the note and put it on his desk, but he seemed somehow lost in the shuttered gloom, as if part of his mind were in the Herzog office, sucked down the line, through Beni Drar and Sidi Bouarfa.

'These women, are they pretty?' He made gestures with his hands to indicate what he meant.

'Société Herzog has only the prettiest,' I said.

'Ah,' he said, as if this explained everything.

'Maybe you could try a telegram. They would have to take that to your friend, would they not?'

'Yes, but Mustafa, the Post Office . . .?'

'Ah, the Post Office is not a smooth pillow for the cheek.'

'It is dreadful.'

'My friend, I am aware of that, but bureaucracy is no respecter of persons.'

I shall not describe the scene at the post office, the queuing, the buff forms on thin paper in three languages, and the lack of order. In the end, a message was sent; a telegram hurtled out along the wires, through the slums, through the lime-treed bourgeois suburbs and the thin scrub by the railway tracks, across the dust plain to Zef and beyond to the capital itself, where it came to Munton's hands.

My message read:

'WHO THE HELL IS ZOBOTI. WHAT RELEVANCE DEAL. BRIEF HISTORY AND ACTIONPLAN SUGGESTIONS DOUBLE-QUICK. NARRATOR.'

I received the answer at midnight, as the Imaam in the mosque was clearing his throat preparatory to the call to prayer. A cry drifted up from the street below, through the French windows, into my bedroom, where I lay trying to sleep, under a single sheet.

'*Monsieur Narrator! Télégramme. Monsieur Narrator!*'

I do not recall the noise of a motorcycle, but as I looked down into the street, through the luminous mist that drifted there, I could see the form of a large pre–war BMW propped against a tree, and the helmeted figure of a despatch rider, foreshortened in the gloom. I ran down the stairs and opened the security door to the cold. The despatch rider was covered in fine dust. One leg of his grey corduroys was torn, as if he had caught it on the bumper of a passing car.

'Ah, Monsieur Narrator. A three star telegram for you.'

And there it was, my reply from M.

'ZOBOTI FRONTIST. DANGEROUSLY EFFICIENT BUT NOT UNGREASABLE. SUGGEST RATSITVOBITALEYDEMEDIAT. MUNTON'

Ratsitvobitaleydemediat? An unpleasant misprint.

THURSDAY 2ND OCTOBER

A day of dreadful events! I suppose really this was the day when everything began, if I try to put my finger on it, though it is foolish to try and do such things. In a way, the roots of it all went back further, but this is the day I think I will remember as the day things became nasty, rather than amusing or quaint (of course these qualities are closer together than one might think).

At any rate, I spent the early part of the morning in my room, with Munton's telegram and some big sheets of blank paper, which rapidly became filled with my theories as to the meaning of his obscurely jumbled final words. I tried every conceivable combination of them. I juggled the letters, I took out the consonants, I took out the vowels, I considered if it were in code (things could be so difficult this could conceivably have been thought necessary — I remembered the way 'the present time' had been underlined in his letter). The more I worked with it the more I became aware of an ever increasing sense of frustration like a knot to which an extra half hitch is added every minute, growing somewhere within me, a creeping sense of unease. The more I concentrated the more irascible and uncommunicative the letters became. The faster and more angrily I wrote the less legible they were, and when I went back over the columns I became confused as to exactly what I had written, and had to start operations over and over again, painstakingly. I abhor word games, and my calculations were made more inaccurate by the noise of some work of demolition going on outside, further down the street. At first I had been aware of a thumping, insistent sound, irregular, as if a pile driver were being operated by a team of day labourers, on muscle power alone. The noise was at once discernible but not clearly identifiable, like a foghorn heard in the distance on a wet and misty day at the seaside. As I worked on at the telegram, the noise became louder, punctuated by the occasional loud crash, as if boulders were being dropped from a height. Eventually, as progress with the telegram eluded me, a rival curiosity took its place, and I left my work for a moment to investigate the source of the disruption. I opened the French windows out onto the balcony and the noise stopped, almost as if those responsible for it were engaged in some illicit activity that they did not wish me to see. I leant over the balustrade and looked down the three floors to the street below, through the branches of the plane trees, which moved gently back and forth in the light breeze. It was a hot day, and I could smell the rubbish left for the binmen at the foot of the tree. Then I heard someone shouting orders, like a demonic bandleader, and a tremendous noise of hammering began, as if pebbles were being fired at a corrugated tin roof by an army of small boys. The noise came from the corner where Repair Man's shop stood. I could see nothing; the tree blocked my view totally. I leant as far out as I could, and briefly caught a glimpse of a large, silent crowd through an opening in the trees. I felt suddenly cold, though the sun shone.

I went down to investigate. When I reached the crowd I could tell that the event involved the Military Police. The numbers watching were substantial, but they were not behaving as a crowd should, neither shouting advice or encouragement to entertainers or jugglers, nor trying to sell things to one another.

Although the crowd was large, the road was still clear and the traffic on it slowed, I saw the nature of the crowd, and accelerated away again rapidly. The crowd was like the crowd at a funeral, or outside the house of someone well-known who is ill. They were quite silent, all looking towards the centre: the grave or the door through which the medical bulletins would come. They were withdrawn within themselves, impassive in the face of the object of their attention. In the centre there was a great pool of silence, deeper than the rest, some twenty yards across, and in the centre of that pool, at the very heart of the crowd's attention, was the Director of the Goughly Military Police, overseeing the complete destruction of Repair Man's bicycle shop.

He stood there, his short legs rendered more stubby by riding breeches pushed into long boots, rocking back and forth on his heels, like a circus barker introducing an act of dubious taste and safety. His greatcoat was pulled up so that his hat appeared to grow directly out of his neck, a headless form, deformed in the sunlight. Three men in grey fatigues were knocking breeze blocks out of the wall, and every so often there was a crash and a block would smash to the ground where Repair Man's brother had played draughts. The fragments of the shattered blocks ricocheted out around the feet of the men's commander. The tin roof lay buckled amongst a chaos of bicycle parts: a blue child's tricycle frame, some old wheels, the spokes rusted. A fourth soldier was loading great festoons of inner tubes carefully into the back of one of the grey military landrovers that was pulled up clean across the pavement. As he emerged into the sunlight he screwed his face up against it and it seemed for a moment that the tubes were intestines, and the soldiers face distorted with disgust, not sunshine.

On the opposite side of the crowd I caught a brief glimpse of Repair Man's brother, the merest glance, as he absorbed in one terrible moment the nature of the day's events. He turned, almost before I could recognise him, and dived out through the curtain of the crowd. I was half tempted to follow him, half fearful, frozen there in indecision. It was a long way round the crowd to its far side, and I was already deep within the perimeter. By the time I had fought my way out, then round to where I had seen him, he could well have disappeared. Perhaps I hoped he would have, perhaps I regretted having seen him at all. At any rate, it was quickly too late ... he had gone, fled. Maybe he was walking fast, but not too fast to attract attention, thinking rapidly, counting money in his head.

Of Bicycle Repair Man there was no sign, and I half feared he lay there under the wreckage, feared to look too closely at the tumbled blocks lest I should see the torn trouser leg, with the leg still in it, jumbled in there with the broken mortar and the bicycle components not worth looting.

One of the men on the wall stopped work for a moment, reached down and pulled out a framed photograph. He tossed it into the street without looking at it and it skidded, splintered, across the road surface. A barely perceptible ripple ran across the pool, between the two sides of the crowd. The commander swung around, his shoulders hunched, a rude hot face, angry at the crowd, at the work, his eyes sweeping across us looking for an individual with whom to tackle the grand collective sigh that had disturbed the calm of his pool. He had an understanding of collective emotions. Then, beside me, I noticed a neighbour from downstairs, one of the French Geologists who were in town with Aramco or one of the other outfits. He was in running shorts, gym shoes, had apparently been jogging.

'Bad business,' I whispered.

'Incompréhensible' he said, and touched the side of his nose meaningfully.

'*La politique?*' he asked, looking away, so that if anyone heard the word they would have difficulty in detecting who had spoken it.

'Probably,' I said. A thin boy in a green tracksuit leaned forward between us, as if on the point of saying something, then thought better of it, and resumed a false nonchalance, blankly staring at the activities before us. From time to time a pedestrian would turn the corner into the street, notice the crowd and the kind of crowd it was, then turn back. Some even made elaborate gestures as if they had forgotten something urgent that required them to retrace their steps to where they had started from. Overhead, the plane trees rustled, a gentle breeze, a blue sky, until eventually I could stand it all no longer: the terrible methodical way the blocks were being dislodged, the hurried urgency of the men completing the task; it was an urgency without hatred or fury, an expressionless urgency, cryptic like the photograph of Zoboti's audience.

I felt vaguely sick and pushed my way out of the crowd. In a way, the open space was worse than the claustrophobic gloom of the place I had come from, one felt more exposed, less safe. All the life seemed to have been drained from the street; by now the traffic had dwindled, the shops emptied, their owners bemused, standing there in the doorways with their thumbs hooked in their belts, looking up the street.

I walked away, with increasing speed, as if pursued, though I knew that it was unlikely that I would be. I remembered an incident that had happened to me long ago, on holiday with my mother in some nondescript town in southern France, when a piece of parapet, decayed by neglect, had broken loose and come down in the street from a great height, only yards ahead of us, crushing a stray dog in its path, quite horribly. There too, there had been the contradictory impulses, the desire to laugh, but of course that had been an accident. Lines led back from what I had just witnessed, back to other events elsewhere, to cool and educated men in white collars in offices where the tea trolleys ran on silent gimbals, and the pay slips were printed by microcomputer. Offices where men, not Gods, commanded events. Zoboti was behind it all in some way; his feet under a brown vinyl laminate desk, his fingers flicking through filing systems sold by men like myself, looking for names worth erasing.

I heard another crash, louder than anything I had heard before, as another block fell, landing on metal, maybe on part of the corrugated roof, and the sound of a crowd perhaps; an angry distant murmur, like the sea, or the wind in pine trees on an exposed hilltop. I could not be sure; it was an impossibility, that murmuring crowd, and yet for a moment, in my imagination, I heard it there. I began to run, and as I ran clear, leaving the noise behind, the life returned to the street. I could no longer hear anything except the normal everyday noises. A horse cart went past, with four huge emaciated drays straining to shift an excessive load of concrete stacked in bags. Their hooves skidded on the tarmac, big veins under their worn hides. Then came taxis, pedestrians, buses, but still I felt unsettled, unnerved by the events of the day. I reached the main boulevard, and slipped into Moriarty's Bar as the clock on the post office struck twelve.

I made for the back room, where it was cool. There was a moist smell of freshly spilt beer, an ambiguous darkness without gloom. The waiter came immediately to me, all white linen and crooked bow tie beneath a pockmarked face, and returned with my beer even before I had settled amongst the elaborate upholstery and gilt of the select room. It was, like all good bars, a place that seemed impregnable. One had the sense that a flick of the fingers would suffice to remove anything or anyone that promised to cause even the most minor inconvenience. Footsteps in the street sounded muffled, as if a strange snow had fallen, a sudden sunshower. The bar was far back off the street, through swing doors, away from all but the off-duty police with their absurd satirical opening lines — 'Monsieur, I too am a Marxist Leninist', like a parody of some Tsarist epoch lost to the memory of most of the western world. I lay back amongst the cushions and considered my affairs, for a moment abstracted from them.

I bought some nuts from a boy, and cracked them between my teeth. In all there was no great loss, maybe there was a gain. After all, no one would believe we had any connection, Repair Man and I. I could barely believe myself to have been involved. Of course one was curious, appalled, even sickened, but then you never knew. That was the crux of it. You never knew, and the more the mind floundered in mystery the greater its desire for knowledge became, and the easier it was to believe that things were planned, that a certain Zoboti, an official at the Ministry, had sent out specific orders. The mind demanded answers, and reality gave them, or suggested them, maybe erroneously. I smiled, and the waiter handed me a note on the back of a section of the train timetable. It was from Murphy, in the front bar. He had seen me come in, and was inviting me to join him.

Now the front bar was different; people drank there to encounter reality rather than to escape from it. The front bar was a convenience bar, for a hurried lunch, a stolen glass, the placing of a bet, while the back bar was for operations of an entirely more lavish nature. I was in two minds, and did not join him immediately.

When I did, I regretted it almost at once. He had chosen a particular corner of the front room where the wall backed onto the steam baths next door, and some of the foetid odour of old steam seemed to have seeped in from there. Here and there, fungi sprouted from cracks in the plaster, and even the picture of the King — inevitably beaming down upon us — seemed coated with a layer of perspiration. The lino was torn; part of it had been uprooted to allow the laying of pipes and had never been replaced. The waiter wore one of those remarkably stained jackets meant for a man of more than twice his size.

Murphy was sprawled out at a table covered with chewed chicken legs and sheets of airmail paper, held down with empty bottles of beer. He greeted me enthusiastically.

'Hey Narrator . . . good to see you . . . shouted at you when you came in, but you didn't hear. Look, I've really got something to show you, you'll really like this. I've been in here all morning working, this is THE place, it's just ideal. I mean the stuff you see in a place like this.'

I tried to sit down, but the chair gave way under me, the legs folding in suddenly, fractured at the joints and irreparable. I took another chair. The floor was slippery underfoot.

Murphy uncoiled another loose bundle of papers and took a great gulp from his beer. The edges of the paper were dog-eared, turned in on themselves, and some kind of greyish scum floated on the surface of his drink.

'Let me read you some of this,' he commanded, adjusting his pebble spectacles on the end of his thin nose. His face was white and translucent, as he fully intended it should be, and benign with confidence in his own cultural worth.

'Croissant,' he began, reading from the text.

'Breakfast,' he added.

'Maybe morning breakfast tiles with newspaper.'

There was a pause, and he seemed to be winding himself up for something.

'And then the nose-pick.' He glanced at me sideways, nervously.

'Y'see, I've been cutting it back.' His hand chopped the air, the name Naima written in blue ball-point across the index finger.

'And then the nose-pick, succulent.'

'That's dreadful,' I said, involuntarily.

'It hangs a surprise on saucer,' he said, apparently spurred by my observation.

'It's a good thing these people don't speak English,' I said.

He beamed enthusiasm, and searched hurriedly for his next sheet amongst the bottles of beer and the chicken bones. I could see the writing on the page was in big letters, as if every new advance required an entirely different handwriting from the one preceeding it.

'What are you trying to do with it? I'm not quite clear.'

He held me back:

'No, wait, there's more of it to come, not much, but there is more. Now listen to this, it goes on "Morning paper, type-faced news, the other world, squared, latrines for the use of . . ." ' He stopped, and looked at me.

'Why's it all so basic. I mean who would read it. What's the point?'

'Communication. You see it communicates, it works,' he said ominously. 'All this delicacy, I can't stand it. We've got to get back to basics, because that's what gets the reaction.'

'But reaction isn't necessarily communication. It's not widening anyone's experience to disgust them,' I argued back.

'Ah yes it is. All this . . . all this filth . . . people should know; they should see it, touch it, feel it as they read. Acne, bedsores, filth, snot . . . yes Narrator, ultimately snot.'

'But they're all juvenile obsessions, not great concerns, they're peripheral.'

'The artist works in the peripheral. We're taught from the earliest age not to venture into it. You've got to venture every-where Narrator. Even into the front bar.' We both looked round to see to what extent the bar was illustrating his point. The proprietor shouted at a man on crutches, who hung

36

suspended by his elbows like a vulture on the steel counter's edge, complaining about his bill. The proprietor's face was blotchy, the eyes recessed in the fat below the lids.

'But the world is nicer without it. I'd prefer tunnel vision,' I said.

'You've got to tell the truth, some kind of truth, that's what it's about. Snow White had periods like any other teenage girl. Probably a lot more besides, what with hanging around with those dwarves of hers.'

'Don't be so childish.'

'The future lies with snot, Narrator, SNOT. Do you understand.'

He had a way with words. First the business with Repair Man and now this; Murphy plunging forward into a new and horrible literary quagmire. He must have seen my expression, because he quietened down.

'Ach, I see your point. See it, but don't accept it. I know you've got to have a readership in mind, but they don't all have to be like you, do they?'

'Its just that it's not my kind of stuff.'

'What is?'

We talked some more, the thin beer turning sharp in my stomach, eating nuts, watching the people come and drink at the steel bar. The cripple fell from his crutches and was thrown into the street.

I told Murphy about the demolition of Repair Man's shop.

'Ach, that waster. He was up to no good anyway,' he said. I went home for lunch.

After I had finished eating, I began again on Munton's message. The business was becoming infuriating, and the lines of letters less than helpful. RATSITVOBITALEYDEMEDIAT. They marched across the page like armies under the orders of an ailing general, defying analysis. I sharpened my pencil gloomily, and a knock came, echoing emptily in the stone hall outside. I had not heard footsteps mounting the stairs. I opened and Murphy's girl stood there, with mischievious shyness, on the doorstep. I could hear the prayers of the geologist's children burbling from below, like a fountain, meaningless and everpresent. When the girl saw me, she seemed on the point of running away, without speaking, as if in the grip of a sense of irredeemable inferiority. However, she thought better of it and said:

'*S'il vous plaît Monsieur. Est-ce que Monsieur Murphy est là?*'

It was almost as if we had never met, as if I had never listened to her needling Murphy, quietly, with determination. Maybe she did not remember. At any rate I was struck by the beauty of her French: the way her tongue tripped delicately along the edges of the words, with every accent receiving full attention, perfectly in place. I said Murphy was not in, but that he was sure to come back later. She smiled, and one pointy toe traced a thin line in the ochre dust on the floor across the hall. I am often at a loss to know what women here are thinking.

'Would you like to come in?' I asked her.

She started, as if the suggestion were suddenly too shocking to contemplate, and turned to look down the stairwell, as if assuring herself that her means of escape were still available. She was very beautiful, more beautiful than when I had first seen her. The noise of the air-conditioning unit rumbling into action broke the silence, a distant sound of switches snapping on and motors starting.

'What is that noise?' she asked.

'Air-conditioning . . . you know . . . to keep the house cool . . . it's automatic.'

'Huh,' she said, as if trying not to be impressed.

'Did Murphy say when he would be back?'

'No, its difficult to say. He's down at the bar.'

'Aaah,' she said, with the same vague disapproval that had greeted the details of the air-conditioning. She seemed for a moment to be calculating. I do not know what it was; perhaps she feared to look at me face on because the figures would show clearly there, in her eyes.

'I will come in and wait,' she said finally, and walked straight past me into the flat, her high heels click-clacking determinedly through the lobby to Murphy's room, where she pushed open the door, without invitation. I felt suddenly invisible, as if watching a burglary but powerless to intervene.

'He's not in, I told you,' I said, but she had already entered. I followed her and stood in the doorway while she leaned over his table. He had been writing letters, and the table was again covered with his sheets of blue airmail paper. The blinds were down, and the room smelt of socks. She turned over the letters with the same slight air of contempt.

'It's in English,' she said. 'Who does he write to? Why do all you people spend such a lot of time writing?'

Before I could answer she had spun round and pulled open the door of Murphy's wardrobe. She giggled and held her hands to her face, like a much younger girl.

'Just look at his shirts, I mean they're ridiculous!' She brought out one of the grey shirts he had bought on his last trip to Lisbon. The sleeve was torn, and this seemed to amuse her greatly. She began shuffling the hangers around in the wardrobe and chuckling as some awful new humorous aspect of his clothes was revealed to her inspection.

'Be careful Maria, he may come back. He won't be pleased.'

'What do I care!' she said, and then sighed, like an actress playing to a small audience in a large and draughty hall. She caught sight of the bed — a crumpled mass of yellowed sheets — strode over to it, and quickly, efficiently, re-arranged it, puffing out the pillows. Then she walked to the window, and let the blind up with a startling rattle, almost angrily, as if the room were somehow being punished for Murphy's absence.

The side of her hair had been reddened by the continuous use of Henna, and glowed in the afternoon sunlight. She flung open the window, and the light curtains blew out into the room in the afternoon breeze. She leaned out to look down into the yard below, wearing tight jeans of a continental cut. She was like all the girls someone else had had in one's teenage years, and for a moment I thought she had leaned from the window deliberately, so that I should think just that one thought. She glanced back into the room once, quickly, as if to see if I had noticed, and continued looking down into

39

the yard. The letters on Murphy's table began to blow across the room, sheet by sheet, peeled off by the breeze.

'Would you like some coffee?' I asked. She turned back from the window.

'Oh no, Monsieur. I think I will sleep until Murphy comes.'

She slid onto the bed, and lay on it, face down, her nose pressed into the pillows, totally motionless. Her shirt had ridden up at the back slightly, and the flesh of her back was brown, with a foreignness about it, against the white cloth of the shirt. I had the impression she had waited often in this way, with a kind of despairing resignation, a hunched attentiveness.

'Can I get you anything?'

'Oh no, no one can get me anything. Do not concern yourself, I will be all right Monsieur.'

'You are sure?'

'Absolutely.'

I closed the door on her, and as I did so I heard the rustle of the bedclothes, as if she had sat up suddenly on my departure. I expected her to call for me to return, to ask for something, some excuse, something; but the room was silent. The thought of her there, sitting upright, listening to my silence on Murphy's bed disturbed me, and I shook my head vaguely in an attempt to dislodge it. When it became so quiet that I thought she would hear my breathing there outside the door, I returned to my room and began to toy disconsolately with Munton's telegram once more.

About half an hour later Murphy came crashing in and I intercepted him before he reached his room. He smelt strongly of aniseed, and had his tie on where his belt should normally have been.

'There's a girl in your room,' I whispered.

For a moment he looked anxious.

'What girl? What's her name?'

'It's Maria.' I said. He looked blank, distracted, curiously deranged, like a cyclist after an accident.

Somehow I couldn't explain to him the odd atmosphere of her arrival, felt guilty about the way I had let her poke around, and guilty about the way I had looked at her.

'What does she look like?'

'You know. You introduced me to her. The girl with the fabulous bum. The one who had a go at you in the kitchen yesterday.'

He rubbed his hand across his forehead, and pushed his spectacles awry.

'Ah, yes! God. Maria. Great girl,' he said. 'You're right about the bum.'

He smiled vacantly, and disappeared into his room. I expected to overhear the sound of conversation, wanted to overhear conversation, but the only sound was the blinds being drawn down and the door closing. The silence continued. It filled every nook, every corner of the apartment, like a liquid flooding under doors and through keyholes, distracting every thought. The silence continued for an hour or so, utterly unavoidable, and while it was there I found that I could do nothing. I kept trying to visualise, to comprehend some connection between them, but it eluded me totally; some way he could have encountered her, some clues to their relationship. The sound of conversation, laughter, sex, argument, each was possible, but not a total silence.

I tried drafting a letter to Munton for clarification, but could not begin to phrase the necessary important questions. I sprayed the room with fly spray, but it irritated my eyes. I leafed through an old copy of Paris Match, and paced out on the balcony. Inside the magazine there was a picture, of a man who had been blown apart in his garage by an exploding tractor tyre, or at least a picture of a few stains on the ceiling, and a simple drawing of how the accident happened. Then I heard the door of Murphy's room open and the sound of footsteps. The outside door opened and closed and a woman's shoes tapped away down the stairs.

In the bathroom, Murphy was bent over the sink, washing his armpits, and whistling some Republican tune between his teeth. Somehow I couldn't ask him anything. He dried his chest, and walked past me into his room.

'Great little girl,' he said, and nodded, the door closing behind him.

Of course, there was nothing I could do. He had sensed my growing curiosity, looked out for it, maybe provoked it. If I asked him now he would grin again and make some remark about her body, which was after all at the root of my curiosity and maybe his. He was in there at his typewriter again, and I could hear the keys rattling, interspersed with a dull thwacking noise each time the T or the F became stuck, as they frequently did. What annoyed me above everything else was the way the girl had leant out of the window, and a vague impression of laughter at the moment when she realised I had been watching, as if her bottom were somehow an answer to the air-conditioning and Murphy's continual writing.

I sat down at my desk. Sheets of paper were showered across it from the morning, covered with possible meanings. There were doodles around Ratsitvobitaleydemediat: clusters of grapes, the beginnings of a Gaudi cathedral, ominously complex. Had I been an English commuter — the mind searching for an escape from petty obsessions in crosswords — no doubt I could have re-juggled the letters. It was not in code. I had written that in the morning. Munton despised subterfuge, as did all people who did not really care one way or another. It must be a simple telegraphic error. I had written that once, fairly neatly, and later underlined it twice. I looked again and the letters formed themselves into TIT and BUM, which I rapidly scribbled on the paper, then crumpled up and threw the ball across the room. Timothy Davey? The name of the sales director of one of my contact firms in Scunthorpe loomed out briefly; a blue tie, unfashionable. As far as I could remember I would only figure on his mental horizon as a brief twitch of the synapses, and a curt 'sort this one out, Dora,' through the intercom. There was no real way Munton could have heard from him. Even if he figured in the message somewhere, that still left the rest of it, the rats part. RATS OBIT, something nasty, something distasteful, like the trouser leg in the rubble, with the leg still in it.

The business suddenly came to depress me, and I felt a sudden shudder, whether through the muscles of my leg or through the structure of the building it was impossible to tell. The windows rattled, as a wild stray gust crept up round the corner of the street, past the debris of Repair Man's shop, already soiled by litter and dogs. My desk was disordered, more than I had noticed or wished to notice. The writing on the pages was haphazard, as if written by someone else.

I decided I had to visit the capital, to visit Tabar immediately. "Visit Tabar immediately", I wrote firmly. Of course, that was it. That was what the message meant. Things are easy to miss, especially when you are looking hardest.

FRIDAY 3RD OCTOBER

I was awakened early on the Friday by the weather. The air in the room seemed unnaturally hot, close, as if a blanket had been wrapped tightly around the house all night. It was dark, and the darkness had almost a soup-like consistency, quite impenetrable. For a moment or so I thought perhaps the flat was on fire, or the apartment below, and the floor was being heated by flames licking against the ceiling of the room underneath, or by smoke that was thickening in the stairwell, the lobby, outside my door.

When I had rolled out of bed however, the floor seemed quite cool underfoot, but some grains of sand had drifted in. I could feel them as I walked towards the French windows, vaguely irritating and barely discernible. At the French windows the sand became thicker, and I stopped for a moment, afraid to open to the outside world. When I finally undid the catches and eased the painted slats ajar, warm, air blew through the gap, mixed with tiny grains of sand; the kind of sand found on the finest white beaches and dried in the dunes by long hot summers. I looked out. There was a powerful wind blowing, and the plane trees in the street were creaking and moaning, their leaves blown back and upturned by the gale. The sky was a muddy, dirty colour against the first feeble glow of the sun, struggling to lift itself above the horizon behind the nondescript bulk of the Intercontinental Hotel. The grit blew in my eyes and I slammed the door and put on the light, though even then the room still felt dark and somehow oppressive. I went to the bathroom and washed the sand from the corner of my eye. One small grain had somehow managed to lodge itself between my front teeth, and I borrowed Murphy's toothpick to get it out. I could hear him swearing in his room, the noise distant, for once subdued.

'Jesus Christ. Well by fuck. Jesus F. Christ would you look at that. By Christ that's amazing.'

His door banged, and I could hear his slippers shuffling forwards to the door of my room, the sound of his knocking.

'Narrator ... you up, Narrator? Hey Narrator, there's a sandstorm, quite incredible.'

I shouted out that I was in the bathroom, and the slippers shuffled back towards me. He opened the door, naked except for a pair of bright yellow pointed slippers. He smelt strongly of sweat, and without his glasses he had an uncertain peering look, quite unlike the air of artistic integrity which they normally gave him. His sweat smelt like some new acrylic chemical, vaguely unnatural and inescapable.

'Hey, have you seen the sandstorm?'

'Yes, probably the end of the world.'

'Wouldn't that be great?' he said, scratching his privates and smiling quizzically.

'I doubt it.'

'C'mon, the end of the world would be just the thing. What are you up to at this hour anyhow?'

'I'm going to the capital,' I said, feeling for a moment a slight thrill of self-importance.

'Well then, its no problem if the world does end down here. You could cancel the trip Narrator. Bumfuck the lift boy in the Hotel Goughly, drink Pernod and orange ... there's any number of things you could do you know.'

I pushed past him into the kitchen, but he followed along behind, still naked.

'You could send them a cable. Tell them you've become a nihilist missionary, gone out to darkest Africa to eat people. I mean Narrator, there are NO KNOWN LIMITS.'

'Maybe I'm one already.'

'Don't be so fucking pompous! What are you going up to the capital for anyway? Some new and exciting capitalistic enterprise? What is it this time? Some little gadget like that trunnel thing you showed me before; metal bent at both ends and utterly useful to no one, a memorial to man's inability to construct universal meanings?'

'Why do you have to be so belligerent in the mornings?'
I asked. He annoyed me, bouncing around the kitchen in
front of me, his fists up like a boxer squaring for a fight, words
tumbling pointlessly from his lips, an empty nattering vacuum.
His organ flapped up and down absurdly as he moved.

'You're disgusting,' I said. 'Why don't you get dressed.'

He grabbed the dishcloth, and wrapped it around his waist
like a loincloth, chuckling.

'Why, Narrator? I mean it's Africa after all.'

Then, he seemed to remember something, and bounded
off to his room, returning seconds later with a thin slip of
paper.

'This is it,' he said.

'This is what?'

'This is the new art form.'

I looked at the slip of paper. On it, neatly typed, was a single
word: MASTAGULATION.

'Mastagulation?'

'Yes, that's it. That's all there is, I mean its really down to
the basic entity now,' he said.

'Well, I suppose it is, but what does it mean?'

'Well, it's not meant to be precise. It's more like a noise
heard half asleep from bed in the morning, or distantly over
a lake. You know, a kind of sonic unpleasantness.'

This time he seemed to have total confidence.

'Where's the rest of it?'

He said there wasn't any more, that that was all there was.
It was the modern art form. High pressure man had no time
for books. As he talked he cut open an avocado for his breakfast, and made himself coffee.

'There won't be book shops now, I mean all that is on the
way out. In a way you'll just write your own book, with this
as a kind of stimulant you swallow before your imagination
begins.' He suggested I should take it to Tabar and think about
it. Not wishing to offend him, I rolled it up nervously into a
small tube the size of a cigarette and put it into my breast
pocket. He hummed contentedly, to let me know that
nothing I could say would sap his confidence, while I nibbled

46

at some stale bread and an old tin of paté. I wondered again about his relationship with the girl, and the sky lightened outside the kitchen window, though still retaining a kind of lowering gloom. The noise of the sand could just faintly be heard, a trickling, tickling sound.

Once I had said goodbye to him I made my way down to the street, my head wrapped in a towel, clutching a small two-night bag and my papers in an old attaché case. On the steps I met the postman, a brown paper sack over his head with holes cut from it for the eyes. He blinked to dislodge sand that had gathered in his eyelashes, and muttered 'Terrible . . . terrible Monsieur,' as I walked past him and out into the road.

Cars zig-zagged towards the city centre, driving slowly so the sand would not dull their paintwork. Their windows were tightly closed, faces peering out at the curiously changed climate. In the residential quarter the successful greengrocers and pastry merchants flapped around in their djellabas, with the hoods drawn up, sellotaping sheets of newspaper to the bonnets of their Mercedes. The terraces of the cafés were empty, abraded clear of people. I caught a glimpse of the head waiter of the Café Rubric desperately manhandling marble tables and wicker chairs in through the plate-glass windows, while great sheets of plastic from the building site further down the road blew past outside, and cement sacks, empty olive oil bottles, driven by the wind and rolling aimlessly. On the corner of Rue de la Gare three vagrants, wrapped in sacking, were bundled up together behind a tin advertisement for orangeade, which formed a partial windbreak against the sand. On the balconies above, women appeared in pink nylon housecoats, slamming the outside shutters, drawing the bolts.

At the station itself, through the brass doors (upon which rampant lions had been cast) I came upon the customary mass gathering there for the morning train to the capital, crushed together, shoulder to shoulder around the booking office. There was some fighting, and I could see bodies, occasionally lifted upwards from the crowd by the sheer pressure of people, fistfuls of money held aloft, orders shouted.

47

The noise was tremendous, and the queue seemed to lengthen rather than shorten before the ticket window. From where I stood, hesitantly, I could not see the slightest crack or fissure in the throng which I could exploit to get closer to the ticket office. It was as if the bodies were welded together against the glass, behind which the clerks worked at a leisurely pace, like rare fish in an aquarium besieged by a particularly large school party.

The moaning of the wind was less noticeable now, behind the doors, though when they opened of course it could again be clearly heard above the noise of the crowd. From time to time beturbanned figures would labour in carrying great sacks tied up with twine, or baskets of half-dead chickens or rabbits, followed by their women, enclosed in white, or black or brown, depending on their custom. Everyone seemed to be buying twenty or thirty tickets for twenty or thirty different destinations, as if the crowd at the station were only the advance guard of another vaster crowd which would arrive later to claim their seats.

Then the noise began to change; a new tone made itself heard, on a higher note, a slight note of anxiety, of anger, then of fear. Then the noise stopped completely except for the cries from those who had been hit as the police came in off the platform, pushing the station officials aside. There were twenty of them or so. Perhaps they had come up the line by train and were annoyed to have found the crowd there, perhaps they had orders to clear the crowd. At any rate they moved outwards into the crowd, poking at people's ribs with their sticks, moving them back, trying to establish some sort of orderly queue around the walls of the waiting room.

The room was mirrored, so giving an impression of space that was illusory, so the policemen poked and shouted and pushed people towards the corners of the room where, in fact there was nowhere for them to go. The buying of tickets stopped almost completely. One older man, clutching a large mahogany wall clock, hooded and shuffling, lingered longer than the police thought necessary, and one of them struck him across the back of the head, maybe nervous about the number of people there in the crowded space, nervous about the way the mirrors reflected back the crowd, doubling and redoubling it out to infinity. The old man dropped the clock and it smashed to the floor. Its face fell off, cogwheels and escapements disembowelled on the marble floor. He fought his way up into the crowd to escape the police, up beside me, then collapsed quite suddenly, at my feet. His hood fell back, and I saw that it was Repair Man, not just an old man (though I had not thought of him as old before) but a man I knew, or had known well.

I cannot describe the shock this gave me, not just shock, but shock and guilt as well. It was really the first time I had seen this kind of violence so close up, so inescapably (the crowd pressed round now). Repair Man was unconscious and the crowd shouted advice, knelt around him. One man produced water from under his cloak, and sprinkled it across Repair Man's face. Others looked down at him, curiously unmoved.

'Lift his head,' they said.

'No, don't move him.'

'Lift his feet.'

'Here, I have some medicine.'

'What about the clock?'

'Yes, he'll want his clock.'

And all the time, I was conscious of the pressure from behind from the police, who paced around, their gait deformed by discipline, in the space their brutality had created. The clock lay strewn on the stone floor, about five feet from the edge of the crowd, a temptation. Somehow the crowd wanted him to have the clock, but were afraid to risk fetching it. Four of the policemen studied the crowd, scanning it minutely as a censor studies a text, daring them to move for the clock.

Then a small boy, one of those boys like a desert lizard, darted out from the crowd so quickly that he was almost invisible. His bare feet slipped on the polished marble, his hands grabbed at the clock, bundling the pieces together at astonishing speed. The nearest policeman raised his stick, strode forward, gathering speed, but the boy was too quick, disappearing into the crowd which opened to let him through, then closed tightly behind him, acting as one person, before the policeman could aim a blow. Only one small piece of clock remained: the hour hand, lying there, pointing out towards the platform. The policeman who had attacked the boy now bent down slowly, picked it up, and tossed it contemptuously into the crowd. It was part of the crowd's clock as far as he was concerned.

The crowd began to move, their bodies beginning to push around the spot where we were gathered looking down at the injured man.

'Be careful there is an injured man here.'

'Move him to one side, Monsieur.'

But as the crowd passed, pieces of the clock began to come to us, passed forward by hand from the boy, and eventually Repair Man's eyes opened, eerily unfocussed.

'No trouble. I give you people no trouble.' He said.

We helped him up, but his legs were splayed out and groggy.

'My clock, where is my clock?'

'Don't worry old man, the pieces of the clock are coming!'

Everyone patted him on the back as they overtook us.

'The son of Driss from Bouarfa has the main spring.'

'No one would steal your clock.'

'Have some water. Here is some biscuit my sister baked,'

'Mohammed says he will bring you the casing later.'

'But I cause no trouble,' said Repair Man again, wiping the blood from his head before it could congeal in his hair, still not aware that I stood beside him.

More news of the clock came to us.

'Herodotus the butcher has found the pendulum.'

'Terrible. I would not have believed it possible,' said Repair Man. Then he recognised me ... and yet he did not.

'It is Monsieur Narrator, no?' He said, as if uncertain as to how a European businessman could have been so close to a scene of such unpleasantness.

'My friend, it is good, yes it is very good to see you. We must sit together on the train. You travel second class?'

I had not intended to, but as the ticket office approached a vague sense of justice, or justice and curiosity combined came over me. Maybe I was not thinking clearly, but when we reached the ticket window I paid for a second class ticket and a sleeping berth on the last section up to Tabar. Repair Man totalled his money carefully, knotted in a red handkerchief.

As we climbed up from the platform into the train I could see that the storm had begun to lift; the sun's heat came through more cleanly, and the sand was evident only as vague scurries, trickles of discomfort where before it had insinuated itself under every possible protection.

We pushed hard to unblock the doorway into the corridor, where half a dozen people had managed to wedge themselves solid, and somehow flooded off down the train, past crowds surging in the opposite direction with an equally furious determination, encumbered by packages and bags required on the journey. Finally, Repair Man wrenched open one of the panelled sliding doors and disappeared from view into an already crowded compartment, where he firmly lowered his bottom onto a narrow space between two men, and miraculously created a space for himself where none had been before, ignoring the protests that arose around him. Then they caught sight of me, the suit seen on the cinema screen, and a space appeared opposite Repair Man on the slatted wooden bench, and everyone shook hands, touched their chests, mentioned the weather and began the business of establishing their respective social statuses by polite enquiries and the surreptitious examination of each others luggage and the cut and cloth of djellaba and burnous.

Then the train pulled away gently with a strangled distant cry from the diesel, carried away in the wind over the scattered shanties by the side of the track, and slowly the town began to drift away. Individual houses with iron balconies replaced dense unplanned conglomerations of private brickwork and yards full of scrap. Empty litter-strewn wastes replaced the cramped complexities of urban life, and the regular tapping of the train wheels brought relaxation. The sky cleared into

51

a washed out blue over the dusty scrubland with the deep brown of the hills slashed across the background, low down on the horizon.

'Well, Repair Man, what sends you to Tabar?' I asked.

He gave me a warning look, a slight inclination towards the left-hand side of the compartment, indicating some threat lying in that direction. I glanced over, but saw only a man asleep, his head thrown back and wedged at an uncomfortable angle. The man was remarkably clean shaven, and his skin glistened against a smooth white collar. He looked like one of those men who travel second class because they are paid to do so from time to time. Repair Man began talking, but in terms of extraordinary vagueness.

'There are certain business affairs, the details of which I am sure you are aware of, which require my immediate attention.' As he talked his tone indicated that detailed enquiries would only lead to his total silence.

'After all,' he continued ponderously 'it is the time of year for such great expeditions; the end of the tax year, the beginning of the new fiscal quarter. The great insurance societies render their accounts at this time. You see how full the train is, it is as if our only crops nowadays are paper crops. We sow our business seeds during the year and gather in a harvest of rebates and allowances in the spring, or some years later, however long it takes. Mind you (and here he lowered his voice to a whisper) there are times of pestilence, even times of *plague*, when the different bureaux are clogged with affidavits and summonses, and the limbs of the state thrash around out of control, their arteries ruptured with an excess of unnecessary legislation.' He stopped, and leant back unhappily, the impression of moroseness intensified by the way he was squashed into his seat, with his shoulders hunched in order to fit into the inadequate space available to him. One hand still clutched unselfconsciously at the handkerchief which held his money. Something in his attitude had changed; there was a slightly disreputable aura about him. He reminded me of a once great building, which had had its foundations shift, and now stood shored up by hastily erected wooden beams, though the expensive shops still occupied the facade for the moment.

'You have plans for rebuilding your premises?'

'Ah yes, of course. I had it cleared because it was far too cramped. What did I want with a little place like that? I mean it was only built with my own hands and the hands of my family over a great period of years. Who needs a building like that, perfectly suited to one's purposes? No, I already have a scheme in mind for larger premises, a new and expanded terrain. The opportunities for reconstruction are excellent, and I have several interested parties, though growth in the bicycle industry is not what it might be, especially when circumstances . . . when circumstances . . .' He looked out of the window at the straggling dried bushes that sprouted untidily by the side of the track, bowing to the passage of the train, then wearily springing back.

'But still, it is good to travel, as travel gives the impression of movement and movement the impression of progress. There is always the relief of things left behind, though they voyage in one's mind just the same of course.'

He looked at me, and for a moment I thought he was blaming me for something.

'You are an educated man, Monsieur Narrator. Maybe you are responsible with all your ideas of progress. If I had no idea of progress I would have no ideas of regress or defeat, and there would be no setbacks, no disappointments, or at least they wouldn't be felt so keenly. It is you people, you've given us this desire to get up and get on, and led us into dangers.' I nodded, not wishing to argue, and he talked on, working something out, not as we do, for the sake of it, but because it had become a necessity.

'Do you know,' he continued 'the population of Goughly is now four times what it was at independence? There are people *everywhere*, piled in, one upon the other. In the medina, all movement is impossible at certain times of the day; huge crowds gather at the slightest pretext, and stand there swaying from side to side, gaping and gawping at each other and not going anywhere or doing anything. It is like an overcrowded house ... people go mad, they fight, they jostle each other. Everything is confusion. My daughter goes to school with boys now. I mean can you imagine such a thing? It is a perpetual worry to me and I have to beat her more and more regularly. It is a perpetual worry that I should be forced to do that in the name of education. Of course the government does its best to bludgeon the right people, to lock up as many people as it can and reduce the population overall, but there's a limit to what these enlightened policies can achieve. They say it is the will of God. Well, maybe it is the will of God, that is what we used to think, that is what God wants us to think.'

'Is that what you think?'

'I don't know. I really don't!' He blurted out the words angrily. 'I am sorry my friend, I am just tired. We must not disturb everyone else with our idle chatter. I do not really know what I am saying. Maybe it is better if you talk, and let me know how your affairs are progressing.'

I told him about Munton's telegram, the jumbled letters, the struggle I had had deciphering them, but he did not seem so interested in the content of the message as in Munton himself.

'This fellow Munton, does he drive a car?' He asked.

'What sort is it? A Ford? A Mercedes?'

I assured him that Munton would have a car, probably a large one, as he changed models frequently.

'Good, very good,' he said. 'Often possession of a car is a sign that one is on the same general level as the authorities, a useful level, a level that does not cause them anxieties, or rather assures them that the person they are talking to will have the same anxieties as they do. Maybe we can work closely on this, together. Of course my cousin must not be mentioned directly, since it will make them guilty. It is never a good plan to mention people who have spiralled downwards to those who have spiralled upwards at their expense, as it induces self-doubt, and of course self-doubt weakens their hold on power; they are wary of anyone who stimulates such undermining thoughts.'

I found myself wondering at the sudden philosophical speculations which seemed to have rooted and grown in Repair Man's mind since the demolition of his shop: the careful logic, the close observation. He had now become indifferent to whom might be listening, and had raised his voice, almost lecturing, not just at me, but at the rest of the compartment, who were carefully keeping themselves folded away from him, their arms crossed, their legs crossed, their mouths in tight lines, closed against the possibility of joining our conversation. It was rather as if some loudmouthed oik in boots and combat jacket were unleashing a string of unprovoked obscenities in a first-class compartment. I found myself warning him to quieten down, to return to grander but less controversial generalities.

Then he held out his hand, suddenly demanding support. 'We shake hands on the success of our expedition.' I noticed his gold signet ring had gone, leaving a white patch where it had been. Then I shook his hand, and he clutched at mine, longer than necessary. I could feel his nails digging in. He sat back, wriggling his shoulders energetically between his neighbours in order to prise back his position, which had been lost as he leant forward to speak to me. As soon as he was settled he closed his eyes, his hand enfolded upon the handkerchief full of money, and then he went to sleep.

I looked out of the carriage window again. It was midday, and the sun was so high in the sky as to be invisible from the compartment, except as a border of blinding white light along the top of the glass. The scrub had vanished and the train now cut across the great plain before Zef: a blasted landscape of sand, littered with curious collections of sharp-edged rock, but otherwise totally flat. Occasionally mirages would emerge, down on the horizon; hugh gothic ministries, the lakes and castles of a Victorian bureaucratic empire, then fade out of view as the train approached, endlessly retreating without excuse or explanation. The track was bad and the train rocked and swayed, its wheels squealing on the lines distorted by the heat.

For a time I dozed vaguely, with my thoughts disordered, half making sense, but truncated by strange objects and events which cut across them, apparently without motive or meaning. The landscape remained unchanged. The man in the corner shifted in his sleep ... the compartment became hotter, seemed more closed in, somehow sealed and airless.

Through my half sleep I could hear a vague scratching, scrabbling noise, somewhere above my head, as if some small animal were trapped in the luggage and trying to get out. Outside, the derelict and burnt-out shell of a legion outpost drifted past and I awoke, somehow tense and frustrated by the unchanging rhythm of the wheels, pressed in upon by two great Berber women on either side. My muscles were coiled for some indiscriminate action, but there seemed no possible movement that I could make. I stood up, but could not straighten my legs fully without catching my head on the overhanging luggage above. The train negotiated a temporary stretch of line, where a swollen *wadi* had swept away part of the route, and I stumbled, caught at a case opposite to regain my balance, and pulled the case off the rack. It fell to the floor, but even before it fell, I could tell that my movements had dislodged something else, something within the case. A dry, rasping, whiskery sort of sound had come from it, and the cause of the noise became obvious when the case burst open on the floor, and I leapt upwards involuntarily away from the lizards that exploded almost unbelievably from its interior. Everyone woke up suddenly. The two Berber women began to scream hysterically, and wave their arms in an intensity of terror that made all movement impossible for them or for us. The compartment was full of the lizards, big red lizards ('magic lizards') which zipped crazily up and down the walls and over the passengers, intensely speeded up by the heat in the suitcase, and confused and terrified by the pandemonium which they had created.

One of the women tried to get to the door (which was now blocked with the smiling uniform faces of a group of fresh-shaven conscripts). The woman's feet seemed to have become rooted, so her body moved forward and her feet did not, which only increased her terror. Someone had reached the communication cord, and the brakes jammed on. More luggage fell from the racks above. The men in the compartment shouted at the women, telling them to shut up, then shouted at each other, and argued about the best way to catch the lizards, while the lizards zipped backwards and forwards, climbed over each other and fell over all of us. I felt one dig its claws in my trouser leg and then run straight up my body with astonishing rapidity, over my face, and then off along the luggage rack. Seconds later another did the journey in reverse, but stopped at my kneecap, immobile and thinking.

Bicycle Repair Man lunged suddenly at my knee, but the lizard was too quick, and scooted away under the seat. The owner of the lizards, a dried up little prune of a man, waved his hands agitatedly in the air with gestures of apology and concern. It was not obvious how he had come to be in charge of a suitcase full of lizards, since he had no idea how to catch them now that they had escaped. The figure in the corner had awakened at last, and quite calmly seemed to be taking control of the situation. He had stood up, smoothed down the white cloth of his jacket with a practised gesture, and, in a small area of calm which he seemed to have created for himself, was peacefully lighting a cigarette with a faintly amused and deprecatory expression.

Another lizard hurtled across the back of the seat and leapt at me, gripping my flies. With an involuntary flick of the wrist I dislodged it, but it then vanished up the skirt of one of the Berber women, who let out a terrible scream, as if her whole soul had been torn from her body. One of the men hit her across the face, clumsily. . . . In the corridor I could hear the advance of the guard.

'Stand back. Make way. Come on now, move it, move along!'

The crowd thickened about the doorway from the corridor as he levered his way along towards us.

The man in the suit was now ready for action, and he wrenched open the door into the corridor and began shooing the lizards out into the rest of the train, under the feet of the other travellers. At this, the owner of the lizards began to protest bitterly, tried closing the door again and then, on seeing one of his reptiles escaping into the crowd, he went down on all fours and tried to follow it. The lizard was moving at speed and a wave of laughter and panic swept away up the corridor marking its progress. The guard arrived and began shouting. Who was the owner of the lizards? Was he aware that it was an offence to carry livestock in the compartments? He seemed curiously unconcerned by the weeping Berber who had been so strangely assaulted and was at that moment sniffing into a small silver phial held to her nostrils by her travelling companion.

However, with the two women out of action, and the lizard man somewhere out in the corridor, the work of clearing the lizards became easier, though for some reason they were particularly frightened by the guard, whose large black shoes blocked the exit, and whose voice boomed, menacing us all with various penalties.

'He's gone,' we said.

'The owner has gone. He is outside.'

The guard turned and headed back up the corridor in the opposite direction to that taken by the lizard man, generating a chorus of complaint from the conscripts, now impatient at the disruption. The two women fell to consoling hugs and murmurs and the train began to roll again. I bent to pick up the suitcase. It was totally empty and had contained nothing but lizards. Inside the lid, against the once tartan lining, was an address label. 'Gordon Maddox, 12 Acacia Road, Manchester 8.' Of the lizard man there was no sign. Bicycle Repair Man smiled stoically.

'To women, they represent evil spirits,' he said.

The man in the corner finished his cigarette, stubbed it out on his shoe with some deliberation and re-settled his head in the awkward position it had had before — angled into the corner of the compartment. Repair Man went back to sleep and the train began to sway back and forth along the uneven track, further from Goughly with every minute that passed.

I reached into my jacket to retrieve a letter from mother that I had picked up from the postman that morning. Read against the background of one's life out here, these letters always seemed incongrous, with their evocation of some nostalgic world, hidden between simple lines about everyday life in England. For some time I had stopped reading the letters, because they seemed to contain nothing of any substance. They were merely one further fantastical intrusion on an already disordered life. Then of course I had had difficulty writing back intelligibly, though I could not bring myself to cut off all communication completely. I suppose revolts are always in some way hurtful to someone, but I was not prepared to make mine more hurtful than was necessary. Of course the whole attitude was pathetic anyway, because, like most attitudes, it became absurd with hindsight. What did it matter if one wrote to one's mother or not? It was more than usually irrelevant when one looked at the faces, blurred by sleep, that jogged and rocked in unison across the compartment, the faces of people whose decisions had a much greater significance than one's own apparently petty postures.

"My dear Basil,

Dear me it does seem a long time since I last wrote to you, though I have had your letter of the 20th September. I do hope you aren't staying out on the beach too long, as you were always a bit fair skinned. Mind you I do envy you all the time, or what I mean is I envy you having all the time in the world to do the things you really want to do. I have been trying to get that green mould off the garage roof at long last, but the stuff they sold me in Binn's doesn't seem to deal with it. The Fergusons are coming on Tuesday (you remember Amanda, who's now got a very good job at Imperial College), and I'm trying to get together something non-alcoholic for Bob, who can be such a bore."

I looked out of the window. The interminable plain still rolled past, with the slowness of all empty spaces, though by now the sun was beginning to turn red and the rocks and stones on the surface of the plain were darkening, their shapes now becoming more sinister, the expanse of the horizon more alarming with the approaching nightfall.

The letter continued with more information, fragmented, reminding me of a vegetable soup, a mixture of inconsequential facts, which taken together, created a bland but momentarily memorable sensation. She had not heard from my brother, though she had heard from Hornby's solicitor about the old hedge in the paddock. She had not been able to find the particular map I had asked her for, and doubted whether it existed, though she had found some woollen underpants at a reduced price 'suitable for the Middle East', which she was sending out to me. There was something of the essence of all mothers in this: the furious determination to buy and send things of absolutely no value or usefulness to absent sons and daughters. She finished with a standard paragraph, which I think had been in all her letters, more or less disguised in some, but always there.

"Now do write and tell me when you are coming home. When will you be finished out there? You know it can't go on forever (I know nothing can), and (I think I've said this before) there's a limit to how long one can pursue the interesting things and ignore the essential ones. There must be something that someone like you could do back here. It would mean making sacrifices, of course, but life isn't always easy. . . ."

I folded the letter away without finishing it. "There must be something . . . life isn't easy . . . sacrifices. . . ." The phrases, jumbled together, formed a great knot in my mind, heard and overhead, read and re-read almost daily since childhood. It was why I was there, in a way, or maybe just the reason I gave myself.

I looked from the window. The scenery had begun to change; night was falling, and the faces of the other travellers lay superimposed, reflected in the window, on the dust enveloping the first straggling olive groves before Zef. The country now had dark slashes of green scattered amongst the brown, the ochre and the black, and the image of Repair Man's sleeping face, the orange scarves of the Berbers, swept over the trees. Outside, gangs of small children were gathering in great sheets that had been laid at the foot of the olive trees to catch the shaken fruit from the branches above. The diesel hooted again, and we prepared to sleep.

SATURDAY 4TH OCTOBER

Sometime around dawn a searing noise, like thin metal being fed through a band-saw, made its way into my sleep. The compartment swayed alarmingly in the half-light, the carriages banging together as the train negotiated the marshalling yards that surrounded the approach to the capital. Muffled curses arose from the sleeping berths below. The compartment had that moist clammy feel about it, that strong pervasive smell that one always associates with overcrowding and a poor night's sleep. The condensation from our breath and perspiration streamed down the cream-coloured walls while the other occupants of the sleeper coughed and spat in the spitoons by the window.

I pulled aside one corner of the linen blind. Outside there was a grotesque industrial plant, glimpsed against the grey sky, all pipes and conveyors, with a vast green drum revolving slowly, emitting purple smoke from one end. The train crossed a yellow canal and plunged into a deep cutting into which people had thrown various kinds of garbage. Then the cutting deepened and we swept into the long tunnel that cut through under the hill on which the city was built, the engine wailing to warn any beggars that might have wandered in there to sleep.

Repair Man slept fully clothed, wrapped tightly in his djellaba, lost perhaps in hopeful dreams. I gripped his shoulder to awaken him. One hand was curled back over his face as if to shield it from bright sunlight, and his movements as he awoke were sluggish until he opened his eyes, when he became suddenly hostile, for a second or so, in an old sort of way one never sees in England.

The rest of us dressed as best we could, climbing over each other to reach our clothes, limbs entwined, elbows down each other's shirtfronts, feet amongst the luggage that lay on the floor. The train entered another cutting after emerging from the tunnel, and with the blind up, I caught a glimpse of two men playing cards in the middle of one of the disused tracks. They played on an upturned packing case. A small bonfire blazed beside them. Then the train left them behind and edged its way up cautiously under the ironwork of the central station. The announcer wheezed asthmatically in the Arabic they reserve for official announcements, fixed all on one tone, and we stepped down onto the platform, yawning and scratching. The station seemed to sway uncertainly beneath me for a moment, my mind perhaps accustomed to the movement of the train.

Repair Man stood quite still, looking up at the station clock, suspended under the gothic roof. The other travellers swarmed heavily laden up the ramp to waiting hugs and kisses and ticket surcharges. The hands of the clock pointed to 9.30, though the actual time was 6.30 AM. I turned back and pointed this out to him.

'No, it is a perfect time. A perfect clock too. The last time I was here it said 9.30 too,' he said, and began walking slowly.

'Its a pity they did not bring you all the pieces of your clock,' I said.

'I did not expect it,' he said. 'After all, an escapement is a valuable thing.'

Outside in the street the universal language of cities had been scrawled across the morning. Everywhere, in all countries, there would be a place like this, with an impressively wide boulevard, a proper boulevard, the King's palace at one end, and the Palais de Justice at the other, both just visible through the morning mist. Maybe there would be other buildings reflecting the necessities of order, or justice, or money, or faith, with the movements of the people re-organised to show them appropriate respect. Here, as everywhere, there was one of those boulevards with wide, white pavements, frequent roundabouts containing palm trees, flowers and fountains that worked. The statues and buildings were clean, or as always, in the process of being cleaned. Flocks of birds circled, drank from the fountains and left their droppings down the fronts of the many banks and fashion houses, while the traffic came in waves. We could hear its dull rumbling on all sides, though the street was empty. Then, somewhere up by the treasury building, the lights changed, the noise grew, and the front–runners came careering into view, followed by a mass of other vehicles making for the next set of lights. For a minute or so the traffic continued until the lights changed, when there was a brief silence, followed by a rush of vehicles in the opposite direction, on the other side of the road. Everywhere, in every capital, the same pattern: on the pavements the same crowds, containing the same pimps, pickpockets and prostitutes, here in great quantities, there in less — in some places disguised, in others not — but always sufficient to create fear and excitement amongst visitors from the country. This civilisation seemed uncertain however, like a film set besieged until the end of filming.

'We find a hotel,' said Repair Man, lunging angrily at a small boy who persistently tried to polish his shoes.

The Hotel Parano was in one of those streets that are so narrow that only handcarts and certain smells can negotiate a passage through them. It was reachable on foot from the crowded taxi stand at Bedou Abbès, through a quarter too commercial to be quaint, yet too quaint to be commercial in any modern, successful kind of way. As we walked along, the traders hung about there in their doorways, like bats, observing our progress. Many were craftsmen of the inter-mediate type, the clock and radio repair men who had taught themselves something of new technology, and spent their hours constructing and reconstructing the future from thrown out and broken stereo systems and alarms. A few goldsmiths and upholsterers survived, lacking the money to move out to wider and more frequented thoroughfares, where people spent less cunningly and more often.

The hotel keeper regarded us with suspicion and insisted on money in advance. Repair Man argued, and the price came down. We filled in the green security cards and I showed my documents.

'Aah! Chipping Sodbury? I have a cousin in Aberdeen,' he said.

The room we were shown was clean, but every surface, every object in it, seemed to have been used and re-used to the point of exhaustion, dirtied or broken, then scrubbed clean or repaired or repainted. The windows opened out onto a balcony and a courtyard. Down below some women were shouting. The iron balustrade of the balcony had been wired together loosely, while somewhere dogs were barking, with monotonously routine aggression.

Later, I met up with Munton in the Bar X. He was the same as ever; imperturbable, apparently indestructible, though slightly more frayed than I remembered. He wore a suit which had once been white, neither cream nor off-white, but now a peculiar sordid sort of untidy white. He had a spotted handkerchief in his breast pocket, but he had blown his nose on it earlier in the day. He smiled endlessly at his own defeat.

'My dear fellow, how marvellous to see you,' he said, shaking my hand. He had fine hands, but they were pale, the flesh milky against the black hairs.

'Too early for a beer?' He ordered before I could reply, shaking hands again, this time with the waiter.

'Dreadful journey, I suppose,' he said. He always contrived to sound interested, an effect of public school education I suppose, or of isolation. I told him all about the lizards on the train and he listened with his head on one side, laughing loudly at the appropriate moment. For some reason I could not seem to fit Repair Man into the conversation at all. In fact I knew that he would not fit. Munton said that the lizard business was most extraordinary.

'It's always been an odd place,' he said, and then slipped into some tale about how he had tried to get a girl on his one and only trip to Goughly some years before.

'When she took her bra off, her right breast had three bloody great warts on it. Can you imagine that?'

I said that I could, and we ordered more beer. We began to talk about business, the very problem that had brought me there. It was easy to lose the thread almost entirely. It was easy to drink beer on the terrace, and the whole affair might seem part of some bizarre dream, or nightmare, in which one was always working yet always on holiday at one and the same time.

Munton pulled leaves off his artichoke ('Fuck business. If it fails, it fails. That's why I'm here'). He dipped the leaves into a small dish of mayonnaise the waiter had brought.

'It's such a bloody nuisance. What do they want a pump-house for anyway? You'd be amazed the stuff they buy. Incredible! I'd booked up for the weekend in the Snassen with Melissa, in a good European hotel where you can do it with a native as much as you like, then all this Zoboti stuff blows up. Incredible the length of time you can spend fixing these things, just to have it all come crashing down.' His monologue was punctuated by sucking noises, as he nibbled at the edges of the artichoke leaves in a lackadaisical way that contradicted the things he was saying. He really did not care that much now.

'What do you know about Zoboti?' I asked him.

'All I know is that when we got him as deputy secretary at importations, they dropped a buff P2 on us about your pump-house deal. It's some political thing. They're a load of swine. Why can't they just let things go?' He ordered another beer and reached into his wallet, which was attached by elastic to the inside of his jacket. From the shiny black leather he pulled a blank sheet of paper, while from his other pocket he pulled a gold propelling pencil. On the paper he wrote. "M. Sbiti, Direction d'Importations, Bureau no 178."

'This is the man you should see. Flexible,' he said.

'What's the difficulty though?' I asked. But Munton had no idea.

'Maybe he's looking for the usual. Maybe he is not. At any rate he seems to have scared everyone else into total immobility. I mean I don't know how important it is to you.' He waved his hands around vaguely, indicating the smart café, the marble tabletops, the sunshine. He smiled again thinly.

'Who knows?' Then he made a sort of throat cutting noise, or maybe a noise like a jet taking off to indicate that it all might not really last at all. He continued smiling to let me know that he did not care one way or the other, was amused

by the possibility that maybe I did. I could not quite understand it, this complete detachment of his. He could turn
himself on and off at will. Sometimes he could make things
sound important, when he knew they were nothing of the
sort, sometimes it was the other way round. I suppose he had
developed this trait of character through his work. I asked
him about Sbiti, and how he could help me.

'What a noxious little man, you know, with one of those
crumpled red suits and a rubberised shirt. You'll like him; a
real twelve percenter. Mind you he's got his flabby little hands
on the pulse of the directorate, if anyone can say its got one.
Funny thing is, I can't get a belch out of him at all. I spent
the whole night with him in the Mauve Room at Lucretia's,
thrusting Pernod down his throat, and he just sat there farting
and saying how sorry he was, and what a bad business that
things had worked out the way they had. You know, the usual
administrative vacuity. I think this Zoboti chap must have
carved someone up because Sbiti kept slobbering about what
a great man he was. "Yees, a very great, very *democratic* man,
Monsieur Munton." You could tell he was scared the way he
was talking, and he kept looking round, as if expecting to
find one of his secretaries taking notes in the corner with
her hair in curlers.

Then, of course, his little piggy brain fixed on sex, and I
couldn't get him to say anything intelligent. You know the
way they grab your knee and say things like "zee woman iss
as mysterious as the avocado ... you know, ... or ze
pomegranate ..." When I dropped him back to Bar es Souk
he burbled out about how sorry he was that he couldn't help
me. I mean he really sounded genuinely sorry, as if I knew
he was infringing some kind of primitive code by taking my
money and then achieving nothing for us.' He fell silent.
I fingered the slip of paper with Sbiti's bureau number on it.
A definite picture was emerging; the patent shoes, the lounge
of the Hotel Intercontinental, or the Lyndon Johnson lounge,
or whatever it was that bought people like these. I felt more
hopeful; Sbiti could be despised.

'Does it not annoy you in the end?' I asked him.

'There would be no pleasure in it if it didn't,' he said. 'It's in the nature of all really satisfying sports. It's a sort of cricket really: long, boring, complex and played to bizarre rules, but ultimately pleasurable.' He leant far back in his chair and looked up at the sky, as if searching for an English rain cloud in the interminable blueness above. Eventually he paid the bill and we separated, shaking hands.

'I must have a massage.'

'Pleasure again?'

'My friend, massage is not necessarily pleasure,' he said, before the taxi swept him away.

I stood on the pavement and the sun reverberated back from the concrete beneath my feet. I felt strangely confused by my meeting with Munton. When he had left me he had winked in a lewd sort of way, and the more I considered his mannerisms, the more they annoyed me. There was something about him today that I did not like, and something about the situation that was peculiarly aggravating. I remembered the way he had sucked on the artichokes, almost noiselessly, and that had annoyed me also, along with the pursing of the thin lips and the flecks of mayonnaise left around the bitter, sardonic mouth.

A large bus droned past, hooted excessively, then swung away around the corner in a cloud of purple diesel fumes and fine white dust. I had the beginnings of a headache, and could feel the tension running taut across my forehead, down my jaw and cheekbones. The conversation came back to me. Zoboti and the pump–house, the little swine in the twelve percent rubber suit in his bureau, wasting time . . . It was all in fragments, and Munton's eating, the chewings, the slight obscene sucking noises were there as background.

I walked without any clear plan at all, aimlessly letting the streets take me away from the Bar X, detaching myself from the process. It was too early to return to the Hotel Parano. The afternoon was filled with a sense of restlessness without any clear object, a generalised dissatisfaction that nothing promised to distract. The ministry would not be open; the bureaucrats would be at tennis or out riding in the hills, or doing a second job somewhere else. Repair Man had gone down to seek out some relatives by the estuary and to find an escapement for his damaged clock. Nothing really seemed to fit or connect in any definable way; objects seemed linked to each other only by their incongrous juxtaposition, events only by their contradictory meanings. Repair Man had no real connection with my business. I felt suddenly that if he had not been struck on the head at the station, I should not have bothered about him at all. After all I had not bothered before, so why should his misfortune have necessarily changed things?

When one is indifferent to something or someone, initially events which would serve to draw one in are taken as a warning, and one usually withdraws, quite consciously. At this moment, I would probably be in some other hotel, having a shave (or being shaved) and looking through the weekend papers for some kind of distraction for the days I would have to spend in the city. Thinking it over, things seemed to have gone awry, very slightly, as if the general passage of my life had somehow been derailed by the strange terrain over which its tracks were laid. My address at this time could prove to be an embarrassment to my business, and yet the business itself was an embarrassment too. It was, I admitted, an organising factor. Even absurdities have a certain worth because they occupy time, because they demand that shirts be washed, teeth be cleaned, that the shoes be polished, and in the end it ceases to be obvious just how absurd these activities of ours are in the first place. And if I had my absurd activities, I am sure other people had theirs. Repair Man was probably at this very moment rooting through a bin full of clock pieces in the back of some jeweller's shop; unwrapping them, fitting them against the other pieces carefully carried with him in a plastic bag. Munton? Well he was in all probability arched on a stone slab in the steam baths, his body sweating with guiltless pleasure, and Zoboti would be forgotten, which was the way it should be.

By now I had strolled down a side street, and found myself before a cinema. It was one of those great shabby concrete cinemas, built in crumbling ochre slabs to accommodate the maximum number for the minimum cost. A long queue of youths and young men stretched away from the grilled and shuttered doors, away and off around the corner under the plane trees. *La Novice qui se Dévoile* was showing again, and the poster, which was torn at one edge, showed one of those crude linotypes of a nun, with her habit raised, suspenders, outrageous high heels and her breasts bursting unexpectedly from her vestments. It was a popular film. In Goughly at least one cinema could be relied upon to show it at any one time. The street blew with litter while the youths laughed and pushed each other about, or bought sunflower seeds, and spat them into the gutter as I walked past.

Later that afternoon I bought a postcard of the blue mosque and sent it to Murphy to let him know my whereabouts, so that he could forward anything that came through to me. I rather hoped someone would come through and send me somewhere else, though I had no clear idea why I should be thinking this. One place was much like another anyway, except that things were just more or less extreme. I sipped at a luke warm coffee on the terrace of the Cafe Musselman and watched a juggler doing tricks with a monkey, ignored by everyone. The sun had drifted away behind some high commercial building opposite. The edge of my tongue was furred, my legs stiff from walking. *Le Matin du Sahara* lay flat on the table-top. Zoboti was in there again, this time in the front row of a group of dignitaries who had been listening to an oration by the Minister for Water. It gave me no real thrill to discover this, though the upside down parrot was once again there on his lapel.

It was then that I became aware that someone had sat down opposite me, and I looked up. For some reason, the sight of the girl frightened me greatly. Not merely a surprise, but a fear, as if she were both there and not there and no way of knowing which was which. It was Murphy's girl from Goughly, and she laughed at me, as if knowing that I could not comprehend her presence before me. Her whole body shook with suppressed amusement, a not quite pleasurable amusement. She sat sideways on to me again, at an angle, so her hair shielded her face.

'*Salut* Narrator. Do you come here often?'

I thought perhaps that she was deformed, amongst my other thoughts. Somehow I did not like the idea that she might have been sitting there watching me thinking, seeing me sad. I said I was surprised to see her there.

'Nothing is really a surprise in this world,' she said. She wore a long mauve kaftan and high heeled shoes. I thought of the film which the boys had queued for.

'So what brings you here? How did you get here? Is Murphy with you?'

'I have forgotten him.'

'I thought you were friends.'

'I visit him, but I do not like him.'

'Don't like him?'

'He is an idiot.' This was said with a tone of utter finality.

'I'm here to see my sister and her husband,' she continued. 'My father is away on one of his trips to Mauritania, so my mother has allowed me to travel and see the sights. I like the capital, it is a considerable improvement.'

I ordered her a lemon juice, but she did not drink it. She played with the sugar lumps in the sugar bowl, and then moved them around between her long painted nails.

I enquired after her sister and the husband.

'I love my sister and her husband. I really adore them and they have such a happy life, with two small boys. The boys are identical twins, Driss and Yusuf, and they have a maid too. I would like to be so happy as that.' She seemed pre-occupied, as if awaiting a telephone call bringing bad news.

'How long are you here for?'

'Oh I don't know. I have to go back to the university soon, and eventually life here will bore me, I mean I know that already.'

'Then why did you come?'

'Huh! I don't know. Why do you ask me all these questions anyway? Can I have a cake?' We went over to the cake counter where, beneath the polished glass, armies of gateaux marched in green and red. She leant on my arm, became childlike, worried about becoming fat. Her age was almost impossible to estimate; at the counter I would not have made her older than 17. She had that pliability in the face of others expect-ations that creates sudden temporary attachments that are disastrous.

We walked out into the street, and she ate the gateau as we walked along, her head held down as she ate.

'Why do you hide your face?'

'It is none of your business! A person can do what they like, can't they?' she snapped, and took her arm away.

'What do you think is wrong with me anyway? Do you think I'm a cripple? Horribly deformed?' I reached to pull the black hair back from her face, but she pulled back, away from me. We walked in silence for some time, side by side, though she was no longer really with me.

'Shall we go down to the river?' I suggested.

'Rivers make me sad.'

Two small boys called out an insult as we walked past.

'Bastards', she said.

'Why do they shout?'

'Who knows? Maybe it is because they are really animals and not people and cannot stop making animal noises. They're all bastards anyway, and their fathers before them. Maybe the whole universe is made up of them.'

This thought seemed to cheer her up unexpectedly; moods seemed to sweep upon her without warning, making one slightly uneasy, as if at any moment she might explode over some triviality, and strike out with her fists, or burst into tears and crumple totally. I talked about my business, because I could think of nothing else that could be uncontroversial; things which interested or involved her seemed dangerous. So we walked, and I rambled on about Zoboti and the ministry, but she did not seem to listen. For a moment I had the impression that maybe she knew all about it already, in general terms. She would nod her head emphatically from time to time, but quite out of step with the conversation. Then suddenly, she interrupted me.

'My God! What time is it?'

I said it was after six. She was horrified:

'Quick, find me a taxi. I shall be in the most dreadful trouble.'

She gripped my arm fiercly. I asked her to stay, but she pulled at my arm, stepped out into the street, waving frantic-ally at a passing taxi that was obviously full.

'I *must* go. You don't understand. It is late and my sister's maid will know that I have been out again.'

At this point we managed to flag down an empty taxi.

'Quickly! Can you give me some money. Where are you staying Monsieur? Oh, please hurry!' I handed her a note which she seized hungrily, crumpling it up into a little ball in her hand.

'I am at the Hotel Parano, but ...'

'Good. Now go quickly,' she said, both to me and the taxi driver. The taxi pulled away and once again I was alone in the street.

Back in the room at the Hotel Parano I found Repair Man crouched over a spirit stove that he had set up in the middle of the patched linoleum floor. He was pumping furiously with a brass plunger set in the base of the apparatus. On top was a tin cooking pot, and, on top of that a steaming colander full of various vegetables. The room smelt of paraffin and parsnips and steam, and the windows were closed. As I entered, a great curling tongue of flame went up around the pot, topped by a column of black smoke which spread smuts along the ceiling.

'Ah, it is you my friend. The machine is not functioning as it should. The valve is probably blocked, preventing the spirit from circulating.' He resumed his pumping, and more smoke and flame ensued, while the stove began making a loud noise, like someone clearing their nose while suffering the last stages of a head cold.

'Maybe it would be safer to do this on the balcony,' I suggested.

'They would not allow it.'

'Or eat in a restaurant.'

'The food one cooks oneself is better.'

He was concentrating intensely.

'Is it safe to be so close?'

He did not reply. He was making some very delicate adjustments to a wire lever that connected with the pipe from the fuel tank, and which obviously controlled the flow of spirit to the flames. Then the noise stopped and the burbling of the pot could be clearly heard.

'Ah, I have it. It must be treated with respect. Like all machinery, it is easily angered by unexpected outbreaks of temper and impatience.' He stood up and brushed the dust off his knees slowly and carefully. He held his hands out to me.

'I apologise my friend, but when I am in the mood for mechanics, nothing will divert me.' I said that I did not mind, though it seemed odd to be cooking there in one's own bedroom. I sat on the bed, and watched him turning the vegetables over in the colander.

'I like it. It is like when I was young and we hunted, my brother and I,' he said, stirring the pot now with the end of a wire clothes hanger.

Later I described my meeting with Munton to him. I explained that I would have to contact a Monsieur Sbiti about the affair.

'He is some kind of minor official there,' I said.

'No one at the ministry is minor, or if they are they pretend that they are not, and try to mess everyone around in an attempt to convince themselves that they have power rather than the appearance of it. You can pour the earnings of a lifetime into the pockets of those men, even the most minor, and still not achieve whatever it was that you set out to do.'

'But you don't know until you try. You've got to try.'

'Oh yes, you've certainly got to try.'

He pulled out a large painted plate from under the bed. I had not noticed it there before, and it suddenly struck me that maybe they expected people to cook in their rooms, and had left the plate there for that purpose.

'Have you had any news of your cousin?' I asked him.

Repair Man's cousin could be useful, indeed at one time before all this, he had achieved great things for me, though I had never met him, never communicated directly with him. To me, he had always been one of those ciphers who fixes things. I had never really considered the implications of this, as at the time I had been busy, widely occupied on business routines. Repair Man however was disturbed by it all. He became agitated as he talked. He had visited his cousin's family.

'They were very welcoming, very friendly,' he said, 'But their knowledge of him had been wiped clean as if he did not exist. Bizarre. They treated me well and we ate mutton, but all the time I felt they were a little afraid of me, as if I had passed through an area where typhus was widespread. Obviously their duty of friendship to a member of their own family was important to them, and they said that often. My other cousins said how good it was to see me again and my nieces poured me cup after cup of mint tea until it was coming straight out of my nostrils. They clapped me on the back and kissed me, shook hands, washed my feet, but at the end of it all I could almost hear a great sigh lift the roof off the house as the iron door closed behind me. "Thank God he's gone! Now we can sleep peacefully." That is probably what they said to themselves. Do you know, they served me on the enamel plates, and the little girls counted the salad dishes every time they entered the room, to check that none had been stolen.'

He began to serve out the food, squatting there on the floor. I got the impression that in a way he had expected this behaviour from his relatives, that he had slipped back into a more primitive life, connected with the stove, his memories, hunting. He pulled out a small twist of cumin, in a paper, wrapper, and dropped it in the stew. We began to eat. He seemed very hungry and ate with his fingers, squeezing the food into balls, then dropping them neatly into his mouth.

'Did they give you any news at all?'

'Well, nothing much. My cousin came to them every Friday in his Mercedes 4L to visit and bring them gifts. He would come regularly every Friday, until one Friday he didn't come. They sent one of the little girls down to his apartment, but he had moved out. The apartment was empty, the door off its hinges and dust all over the floor as if it were scheduled for demolition and hadn't been lived in for weeks, or even months. There was no furniture and no sign of him, not even foot prints in the dust. He had given no indication of any problems. He had not smelt of alcohol or perfume, and his appetite had always been good. He had continued to offer them Dunhill Gold Filter cigarettes right up to the moment of his vanishing, and was planning yet another trip to Lisbon. Then he just disappeared. His relatives seemed to want to positively discourage any more speculation. "Have some coffee," they said. "Let me fill your glass. Who knows about these mysteries?" Anyway, it makes no sense, like a French administrator. My cousin was a young man who enjoyed travelling, who enjoyed what power and influence he had and used it widely for the benefit of his friends and relatives, and the country. I explained all this to his family, but they seemed quite anxious to quieten me. Maybe in a way they were trying to avoid being caught up in it. I suppose they have succeeded in that, I mean there's always a chance that they have. We are not yet in the age of the efficient tyranny where all decisions are inexplicable, irrevocable, and continued through to their logical conclusions. I think perhaps part of it is grossly unjust, as it punishes the innocent and leaves the guilty. A part of me would today like to see my cousin's family punished too for their indifference towards me, but then that is just a twisted thought brought about by my own misfortune. Ah well, at least it is no longer in my interests to repress my dislike of the whole process, since I am no longer a part of it. I feel healthier out here in the clean pure air of the crowded hotel room, crouched anonymously over my meal.' He smiled, and for a moment I no longer felt a part of his affairs. He said we had to become hardened, and when he said that I became alarmed. I was again included in a plan not of my own making. In fact it was worse than that, because I was becoming part of a plan drawn by someone

I did not fully trust. I asked him what he had in mind, as he seemed on the verge of some kind of action.

'Tomorrow we will go to the ministry. We will see your friend Monsieur Sbiti. If he refuses, we will follow him to where he drinks or whores or takes his bath, or whatever these people do after work.' He seemed to be adopting a protective, organising attitude to my work, taking it over in some way, implying that a mere foreign businessman would have no understanding of his country's processes and procedures. In this there was a hint of satisfaction too, as if he were rediscovering his self-respect in the operation, and that of course made it more difficult for me to slip away from him, to disillusion him again. I could imagine Munton; he would say 'These bastards can be OK, but don't get too close.' He had a vast compendium of contemptible rules of thumb which preserved the pattern of his life from inconvenient interruptions. 'Because they have nothing, one always has something to offer, and the man who has nothing will do anything for the slightest reward, but of course they should be kept out of any high-level business.'

At this time, I could not fully escape the temptation in Munton's rules, though obviously there was little other than self-interest in them. If I went to the ministry alone, I would undoubtedly have more chance of concluding my business.

'Yes, what we must do . . .' he was saying. 'What we must do is go to the ministry, tomorrow, you and I.' He was cleaning the plates in the sink, and for a moment noticed my hesitation.

'You are not happy with my scheme?'

'Of course I am,' I said.

SUNDAY 5TH OCTOBER

I was awakened by a faint whirring noise which began gradually, then developed in intensity, before fading away, all in the space of 30 seconds or so. At first I thought of some insect, a large blue moth perhaps, trapped behind the peeling shutters, then realised that the origin of the noise was mechanical; it had too much symmetry about it. A distinct cranking noise followed as I raised my head from the pillow. Repair Man was sitting on the end of the bed in his nightshirt, like an illustration from a book of Victorian journeys. The crumpled blankets from his bed were strewn with pieces of his clock, like an inventor's midnight feast. He had dismantled the mechanism, apparently with the aid of a penknife, and was checking it through with minute attention to detail. The minute hand alone was attached to the machinery, and the face had been taken off, so the single hand surged around in space, apparently unconnected with any idea of time. It circled around with a uniform acceleration, then slowed with an equally uniform deceleration. Repair Man was utterly engrossed by this, and wound the clock up again hurriedly and set it on his knees where he could see the hand revolving. Each time it came to a halt, he would repeat the process in an apparently purposeless way.

'Good morning Repair Man,' I said. This startled him, and he looked at me guiltily. Quickly he picked up the penknife and began undoing an octagonal brass bolt on the backplate. He looked tired.

'Progress?' I asked.

'Oh, it will take time. I will have to make an escapement. It is a remarkable thing.'

Now that he was aware that I was watching, he seemed to have lost interest in the thing. He wrapped the pieces in a pillowcase and put them carefully away at the bottom of the cupboard where he kept his spare turban.

At breakfast, the hotel keeper brought me a letter. He looked at me scornfully as he handed it over, with more than the contempt of the busy man for the idle in the way he tossed it down amongst the breadcrumbs. It was as if he found it distasteful in some way. It was in a large mauve envelope, and on the front, misspelt, my name had been written in a tiny obsessive hand. In the top left hand corner were the words *Par main*, underlined twice with a ruler. I held it in my hands for a moment, quite baffled.

'Ah, now you have a woman writing to you,' said Repair Man, slurping coffee loosely from the edge of his bowl. Inside the envelope there was a single sheet of paper, also mauve and scented, with the edges scalloped. It was covered with the same tiny obsessive script, so small that it was difficult to read. There was no address, and the letter was in French.

Dear Narratore,

I tremble at the thought that I have the courage to write such a note to you, a near stranger, but I cannot deny the promptings of my heart in this affair.

Narratore, I cannot sleep at night for thinking of you. When the birds are silent and the moon is up, I long for you. This life is so miserable, empty and grey.

Narratore, please, if you wish to speak to me, meet me at the fountain on Boulevard du Pape. When you see me do not speak, but follow me. I await you at 3 PM.

Yours for ever,

Maria

When I had finished, I nearly handed the letter over to Repair Man, but thought better of it. It was so unlike anything I had ever received before, and I found myself wondering whether it was a parody or some kind of local seriousness that I had not yet encountered. It was unexpected in a way, yet she had asked for the address, she had intended it to happen. I turned the page over, but there was nothing on the back. The scent was sickly, somehow incriminating in an odd sort of way. I hesitated to put the letter away in my inside pocket, yet felt that if I did not Repair Man would try to get hold of it to read. Now that I was sure that it was real, I did not want that to happen.

'It is from a friend,' I said, trying to look as if the mystery was cleared up, though the scent still lingered around the table. When I went upstairs to collect my papers and files for the visit to the ministry I took the letter out and read it again. I doubted that it was entirely dishonest, as parts of it indicated a clear intimacy, a clear sense that these words were for myself alone.

These thoughts returned to me later as we walked towards the ministry; Repair Man striding along briskly at my side, talking incessantly about the subtle niceties of social intercourse with Sbiti.

'Now if he offers you a cigarette, you must take it. I know you do not smoke, but we must be careful. Always encourage him to talk; if we can make him talk he will give things away which he does not intend. Ah yes, and stand on his left,' he continued, constructing complex strategies in this annoying way for some time, the breadcrumbs from his breakfast still lodged in his beard like parasitic bugs. I told him to shake them out, which silenced him for a while, but then he started again.

'I am sure this Sbiti will know something of my cousin, but we must not mention him by name, otherwise he will become very wary and reveal nothing. I suggest we talk in terms of the most massive generality.' Sensing my increasing dissatisfaction, he said quickly: 'But of course your business affairs will come first, my friend,' and seized my arm.

At the head of the boulevard lay the ministry, squat and white in the sunshine. Even from half a mile away I could see the crowd waiting for the great gates to open at ten. I felt momentarily anxious, and envied the people on the terraces of the cafés, sunning themselves like chameleons upon the freshly watered tiles, decanters of cut glass and iced water on the tables before them. The nearer we came to the ministry, the more attractive the café terraces became, until the very last café, which had pure white tiles and gilded tables in a fake rococo style, with everywhere the glint of gold on wrists and pendulous against hairy chests.

Then we came upon the crowd and began to move through its outer edge and up to within sight of the gates themselves. Repair Man fell silent, looking at the massive iron doors, and the guards in crimson robes checking their watches and swinging the keys back and forth on long chains hooked to their belts. Every person in the crowd had documents of some sort: fistfuls of papers, wallets full of passport size photos, bundles of affidavits, yellowing and tied with elastic bands or sealed with tape and red wax. Various traders had set up their stalls to deal with the different kinds of business that were created by all this administration (*Photo Officiel, 3 Dinars*), while a translator perched unsteadily on a folding stool holding a placard, on which were displayed his various diplomas. There was a line of writers and typists, before make-shift desks, and the rattle of the keys came intermittently to us through the morning air, together with snatches of conversation.

'But you have brought the *certificat* haven't you? What about the affidavit my friend? Mechtal had clearance in two years, which I find astonishing ... and then, can you imagine it, they said the paper was forged, so I had one forged and they accepted that as genuine! ... it is my fourth visit in three months ... I cannot leave my sheep ...'

The time for the gates to yawn open came and went, and the sun rose higher in the sky. People ate long French loaves spread with honey. The smell of *kif* drifted across and the officials stuck their noses through the bars of the gate into the silent interior of the ministry, searching for a sign perhaps, maybe even a handkerchief waved behind a leaded upstairs window. A fight broke out. Rumours erupted: that the King was ill; his physician had flown to the palace in the mountains, that there was a strike by the telephonists, that the usual leaders had been gaoled until they admitted Russian funding. Everyone was there; men in European suits with brief cases, standing slightly apart, or leaning on the bonnets of large black cars, smoking and watching. Berber women brewed tea, their faces blotched with disease, strange patterns tattooed on their forearms. People greeted friends and relatives, drawn together from opposite ends of the country by administrative necessities, sucked in by the great draught that burning paper always seems to create.

Then at length a voice echoed from somewhere within the inner courtyards.

'Open the gates to the people,' it cried, and the four officials dived forwards, unlocking and swinging the gates open, just as the crowd came upon them. They ran ahead of us, ahead of all the racing people, through the carved and arched entrance and away into the cool interior before they could be trampled. We found ourselves running too, into a grand central courtyard full of tropical plants, with a fountain playing, then through another archway into another courtyard, again with a fountain, but this time crowded with banana trees. We went up some stairs and along a balcony, and the crowd thinned as we went. Some dived through the grey numbered doors that led off the balcony at uniform intervals, while the fittest supplicants leapt up the steps to the second floor. Below in the court yard, the slower and older members of the public were preparing to ascend. We tackled another corridor, a set of steps and then — like life inside an Escher print — inexplicably found ourselves back at ground level in the same courtyard we had started from. Everywhere people were climbing, descending, running, even sprinting along balconies but never apparently reaching their destination; a prized position at the head of the particular queue they had come to join.

Repair Man wiped his face with his spotted handkerchief, his breathing grating in his chest, and we began to seek out Monsieur Sbiti according to a definite system. The grey doors were numbered and inside we could hear business being done in low murmurs and angry rumbles. Queues were widespread, endemic. The importance of those behind the doors could only be guessed at by the faces of those queuing; as some laughed and joked and spat. Maybe some of the doors were munificent, because everyone queuing there before them was happy, while other doors seemed to barely contain some kind of trial, as those emerging riveted the attention of those still waiting.

'How did it go? What mood is he in?' the people asked. Still others seemed to require the completion of dossiers of tremendous complexity, for the queues had great cardboard boxes of papers at their feet, the people there checking the documents off against lists of what was required.

We found the corridor with bureau numbers 150 to 190. The bureau of Monsieur Sbiti — number 178 — was missing, as were the bureau on either side, numbers 177 and 179. Some doors had no numbers at all. Four rooms carried the same number. Finally, we came upon 178 when we were least expecting it, between number 27 and 28 on the third floor, in a quiet backwater of the building. We hesitated, knocked gently, and entered.

Inside sat three women, knitting. A vague and endless Arabic tune wound around the room from a casette player at one of the desks. Each of the other desks had a typewriter on it, with its cover on. The women were all heavily made up and plump, and a faint smell of overheated elastic under-garments filled the room. Repair Man stood deferentially behind me, although it was his country. In fact I had remarked that the deeper we had penetrated into the building, the quieter and less obtrusive he had become. The women peered round me at him, and he moved sideways so as to regain his cover. One of the women continued. knitting in an angry and contemptuous sort of way.

'Is Monsieur Sbiti available?' I asked.

It was difficult to concentrate as the secretaries craned their necks back and forth, seeking a clearer view of my companion.

'Who is your friend?',

'Yes, who is he?'

'Ah. This is an acquaintance. He is here to explain anything that I might not understand.'

'I am afraid Monsieur Sbiti cannot deal with acquaintances.'

'Yes, that's right, he cannot deal with acquaintances.'

They were both slightly insolent in their approach, as if desiring to provoke some kind of minor scene as an excuse to eject us. As far as they were concerned it was not entirely right that we should be together, and anything not entirely right was to be thrown out. Maybe they had been told that.

'But Madam, I am a business acquaintance of Monsieur Munton.

'Indeed,' said one, her crimson lips moving over yellow teeth.

'*C'est pas normal,*' said the third one, speaking in a whisper from her knitting, as if to remind the others of their duty.

'Is Monsieur Sbiti in?' I asked.

'Occupied.'

'Busy.'

'In conference,' they said.

'How long will he be?'

'Who knows?'

'An hour.'

'Maybe two.'

The music wound on through the room. The air was dry, like paper, and I realised my shirt tail was out. Then a door at the back of the office swung suddenly open, to reveal a stubby little man with a grey cannon-ball face, pitted with the reminders of an acned youth. What hair there was on his head was slathered down with some kind of powerful hair oil, and he ran one plump pink hand vaguely through the few remaining strands, momentarily baffled by our presence there. A digital watched beebed mournfully on his wrist. I felt cheered by his appearance: by his crumpled red suit in the latest style of three years before, by the fact that our arrival seemed to have upset him in some way.

'Aaaaugh,' he began, in an attempt at a sound of pleasurable surprise.

'*Aaah, quel plaisir! Quel grand plaisir!* It is Monsieur Narrator, is it not, the friend of Monsieur Munton? What a delight it is to meet with you men of business from Europe.'

One had the feeling that perhaps he had just been interrupted during a particularly intense period of masturbation.

The women, meanwhile, returned to their knitting humiliated. As he came across the room towards us, he let his hand run idly across the shoulders of the secretary nearest to him, and the short little fingers caressed the nape of her neck briefly while she simpered surreptitiously.

He shook me by the hand, then saw Repair Man, who had squashed himself down in a black vinyl armchair which had been left in the corner, for the use of ministerial supplicants. He seemed somehow to have folded away his entire natural presence, to have sealed his charisma away within a large brown envelope, where its light could no longer be seen or noticed.

'And who have we here?' asked Sbiti.

'This is ... uh ... this is a man from Goughly who has some business with you and who has agreed to help,' I said.

'*C'est pas normal*,' whispered the knitting secretary. Sbiti's little black eyes looked at me.

'Well, we need not bother about him. I am sure that we two can settle our affairs amicably enough. Come with me my friend, into the inner bureau.' Repair Man slumped there wordless before me, and then Sbiti took my arm, reminding me for a moment of the kind of grip used by bouncers in smart bars, and he steered me past his secretaries, who now smiled. The office door gaped before us both. At that point, I deserted Repair Man.

The room was spacious, but almost entirely vacant. A large desk in artificial wood sat facing the door, and behind it, a stainless steel swivel chair with black imitation leather padding. The padding had been inexpertly patched with black tape at some point in the past. The desk was bare except for a blotter, a pen holder and a pen; the blotter however had a crude drawing of a woman scrawled across one corner. He directed me to another swivel chair, stationed in a wilderness of pink carpet some 15 feet from his desk. As I sat down the chair rotated uneasily beneath me.

Sbiti paced over to the window and looked out for a long moment. Across a yard, another office could be seen, apparently identical to his own.

'*Bien*, Monsieur Narrator, what is your problem?' He began peremptorily. I explained the necessity of clearing my export order, the essential value of pump-houses to the economy, to his economy, to ours, but somehow my words were muffled by the thickness of the carpet, and I sounded wholly unconvincing. Of course the more unconvincing I thought I was, the more unconvincing I became. Perhaps the whole thing was set up to bring on just this kind of feeling, to test the resolve, to sort the enthusiasts from the men of routine.

Sbiti swivelled gently from side to side on his chair as I spoke, with his head thrown back in the necessary angle of contempt. The distance across the carpet seemed an insuperable obstacle to communication; Sbiti's face formed itself into a vaguely smiling blob on the periphery of vision and, even while I talked, I found my mind going back to Repair Man, and the scene in the outside office. Munton, when I had first arrived, had advised hatred as the very best approach for dealing with these men. 'Focuses the mind wonderfully, and when you despise them and hate them openly they take it as a sign that somehow you have more influence than they do. It's all a matter of subtle intonations which do not overstep the bounds of politeness.' I began to put my case for the absurd pump-house more strongly.

'So, you see Monsieur Sbiti, these clumsy and obstructive restrictions on the trade of free nations could well have repercussions on other orders in your country.' I put as much contempt into it all as I could, trying to accuse him as subtly as possible of backward and retrogressive policies. ('These little swine hate it if you tell them they're behind the times'.)

Sbiti however remained silent, sucked the end of his pen and picked his nose, disconnected in an odd sort of way from the whole discussion. Maybe his French wasn't too good. The air-conditioning system started up, and I could barely hear his reply. It seemed couched in some dreadful administrative language, with great gaps and chasms dividing phrases from each other and words of such vast generality that his meaning was swallowed up in the vacuum that they created in their path.

'I am sorry that these affairs have somehow placed diffi-culty in your way, but you must understand the situation we are in. There have been some important changes and some other things have not changed. Of course, the essential thing is the changes. Yes, changes have been made, and the policy of the ministry is, I am afraid, not what it was. For example, or to show you what I mean, we now find that particular fields of activity are not as permissible as they once were. You must have heard of the currency crisis? I mean really I should not be telling you this. In fact you are unusually privileged that I should be here at this time before you, when many aspects of our policy are up for grappling as it were. . . .'

'So the pumping station is definitely not acceptable?' I asked.

'Well, pumping stations and all aspects of the medium range infrastructure, plus agricultural technology, have undergone changes of policy.' Every time he said changes of policy now he said it with a tone of considerable regret, as if he personally felt to blame, or perhaps because he hated saying 'no' above almost everything else.

'So, who is behind these changes?' I asked.

'Ah yes, the changes . . . well of course there are various organs, various bodies who may possibly be responsible, though of course not everything has been altered. I mean for example, wine presses are outside the present reorganisation. This pumping station, it can in no way be connected with sporting activities? No, well I thought maybe not. We've all got to move with the times you know.'

'But who decided the changes?' I pressed on.

'Well, it may be the interministerial committee, or the bank directorate or, in the strictest confidence of course, it could be the King himself, or someone in the ministry here. Responsibility is really often difficult to pinpoint, especially when there are frequent changes of policy.'

'Zoboti?' I suggested.

'Aha! You have heard of him? We have such a man. He is a very great man, a man one cannot footle about with at all. He makes the rules here now and we go out and bust up the people that break them. When Zoboti wishes to kick someone, we do it. To put it bluntly, we are really only his right foot. He is a powerful man, and his cousin is known in circles of the greatest elevation and obscurity.'

By now Sbiti had swivelled right round in his chair so that his back was facing me, and he seemed to be talking to no one in particular. His tone had become one of gloomy awe.

'Of course,' he added, 'You could always fill in a *déclaration des impôts sur vos revenus des capitaux mobiliers*. It is one of our better forms; and then, who knows? In a year or two, or maybe three, you might have some kind of luck.'

'And with this Zoboti,' I asked, 'There have been changes of personnel?' He stopped swivelling, in a position where he could face out through the window.

'Of course, it is quite normal.' He faced me with a sudden broad smile. I noticed one of his front teeth was solid gold, and for a moment it flashed in a stray sunbeam that cut across the room from the window.

'People have been displaced?'

'Regrettably, but then that too is quite normal.'

'Where do they go to?'

'They are re-located, sometimes permanently, sometimes not. They do not concern you, as their names are no longer on memorandums, though they crop up from time to time on forms delayed in the administrative process.' He smiled re-assuringly, and clasped his hands firmly in front of him on the vinyl desktop.

'My friend outside. He had a cousin who worked here.'

He interrupted me.

'Well, you know ministries are large places, and people become lost, it is not really my affair. Perhaps he has been mutated or relocated as I say. I mean, who knows? It is nothing to do with me, you should not concern yourself with such people. Now that friend of yours, that Monsieur Munton, there is a man I can deal with. Yes, he knows the rules. Its most important to know the rules. People who do not have troubles. Yes, all the time, you may not believe this. Now that

Monsieur Munton, he had the right approach, up to a point. He was not prepared to go the whole way, maybe because he did not care enough about your deal. Perhaps that is something you can discuss with him. Maybe it is his civilisation and that is what stops him. I often think civilisation and business do not go together, don't you? Hah! You see I've become a philosopher!' He rose from his swivel chair, and moved to the front of his desk, where he sat informally, one leg swinging to and fro. I noticed that he had chewing gum stuck to the sole of his shoe. He held his hands out to me in much the same way as Repair Man used to do.

'My friend, do not look so serious. After all, this life is not a serious business. Maybe you will come with me tomorrow to my club. It is very select. Maybe we can discuss your business there with more success. You know, in these surroundings I feel a little constrained; you know one cannot operate as freely as one would like.'

Of course if I refused it would cut me off even more, as he would take it as a slight, take it that I had decided he was too unimportant to trifle with. He could begin to work against me (assuming he was not doing so already). On the other hand if I accepted, it could well mean an exasperating afternoon spent swilling ice cubes around in strong drink and paying other people's bills in an endlessly unproductive kind of way.

'It will be a great honour,' I said, though I was unhappy about the chewing gum. He was not important enough to have been told about it. No minion had leant over and whispered to him. He did not really even seem to deserve his large, empty office. For one strange moment I suspected a vast hoax; that the real Monsieur Sbiti would come bursting in laughing, covered in paper streamers.

'Ah, the bell,' he said, hearing the notes of a distant hand-bell. It was time to close for the day, and a genuine smile crossed his face, his front tooth catching the sunlight again, momentarily blinding me. He walked towards the door, then a thought came to him. He lowered his voice. 'Do not bring your friend. Of course it will be most difficult, but

I am sure you can understand this.' He patted my shoulder, condescendingly.

Outside, as I made the final arrangements with Sbiti, Repair Man hovered urgently, his anxiety to learn of his cousin's fate seeming to overcome the lack of confidence that had struck him earlier. When finally we shook hands with Sbiti (only briefly in Repair Man's case) and went out onto the long grey corridor, he began to fire question after question at me. Had Sbiti known his cousin? Did he know what had happened to him? Why had people disappeared? I tried to answer, but could not, as Sbiti had told me nothing. As this fact dawned on Repair Man he began to brood, silently.

'These people.' He said at length.

'You did ask him all this?'

'Of course,' I said.

He fell silent again and we went out through the great archway into the main boulevard, past the café with the white tiles, now crowded for lunch.

'This business of yours, it's important to you?' he asked.

'Yes.'

He spat angrily, and kicked out at a stray dog which crossed his path. The dog snapped back at him, showing yellow disjointed teeth.

That night he went out alone and returned late with a small piece of fine brass and a broken nail file. He unwrapped the clock and took out the rolling wheel. Then he began taking a series of measurements, and finally started filing away methodically at the brass, with minute, careful movements. I thought about Maria, then went out for a walk, returning in the early hours to find him asleep, snoring obscenely, with one hand over his face. By the bedside there was a small piece of brass, neatly filed. It was the first step towards the new escapement, and the rebirth of his damaged clock.

MONDAY 6TH OCTOBER

Over breakfast the next morning Repair Man glowered. He ate it as if he were alone, and I had to keep reaching across the cluttered table for the butter, the sugar or the croissants. He immersed himself totally in the day's edition of *El Zif*, plunging determinedly through the agricultural and religious pages despite their total lack of interest. Occasionally he would chuckle, or turn the pages noisily. The paper was just too far away for me to be able to read the rambling arabic script.

'What are you laughing at?' I asked, but he did not reply. I found myself again considering ways of transferring myself out of this situation, of changing hotels, of moving, if necessary even at night.

Eventually, when there was nothing left in the paper for him to consider, he folded it carefully and placed it on the table amongst the debris of his breakfast.

'So,' he said. 'I imagine you will be seeing our Monsieur Sbiti alone today.' In a way it was both an ultimatum and a question. We began to argue about whether he could come or not, in the way of people who are already aware of all sides of the issue, having argued them to themselves beforehand. He did not trust me, I did not think it would be helpful to have him there and so on. Then we began to annoy each other with the sheer persistence of our respective positions, as one dog barking at another will do.

'I know. The life of my cousin it is just all business to you. He stands in the way of making money. You and your European suit and your fancy French, you'd rather sit there and suck cock with Sbiti than help out a friend who has helped you before. Mr. American. Mr. Ten Percent.' The sudden change in his manner was shocking, the sudden abandonment of any kind of mutual trust or friendship. I realised that his deference to me was in fact conditional on my willingness and ability to help him, and stood up. As I left him, I caught a glimpse of the hotel keeper, looming in the shadows by the coat stand, looking on with one of those strangely all-knowing hotel-keeper's smiles. It was a faint, barely discernible, mocking smile.

'You can fuck off too,' I said, and ran down the steps out into the street. As I walked away I could think only about the very inevitability of it, the absolutely frustrating, totally fore-seeable quality of the row, the way it was constructed like an ebony box that would fit together and come apart only in certain ways, a puzzle with only one possible conclusion.

I walked on, once more in no particular direction (for the city had none), and the alleyways began to constrict, the tarmac became patchy, then became cobbles, then became mud or baked earth and the sun no longer penetrated. The way began to plunge downwards towards the unseen sound of rushing water, somewhere in the heart of the city. It was an insidious sound, present only at odd corners and turning points, until I could almost feel the spray of fresh water on my cheeks, and yet not see it. 'It is only because I have had too much time to think that this upsets me,' I thought to myself, pressing myself against the wall, feeling its mossy dampness against my face as a donkey laden with ferns came labouring up from the heart of the old town, its owner pulling it by the neck, its head twisted round. I realised I wanted to be back in England. There was an air of unrealism about the place, not unreality, but unrealism. It did not look quite like the sort of place which could or should ever have existed anywhere, and yet I was quite sure that it was there before me. It was like a poorly made set for some play, the surface of the thing was there, it could be touched and felt, but those things that would make it appear credible to the eye or the heart were not.

I descended further, until I reached a point where the path dropped away so steeply that the cobbled surface had had steps carefully set into it. The steps had been secured with iron stakes, to prevent them falling away down the hill as the centuries passed. I had negotiated a score or so of these steps when I saw an incongruous figure like myself, besuited, with polished shoes, picking his way delicately up over the cobbles, fearful lest the leather soles should lose their grip on the wet stones. I recognised him vaguely, even at some considerable distance, but could not remember where I had met him. It seemed as if we had talked, held a conversation of sorts, perhaps shared a beer. I was certain that I knew him as he came nearer, carrying a large brown briefcase with some initials embossed on the side and a brass catch, like a London civil servant. He was using a walking stick with a silver pointed end to lever himself up the steps, inserting the tip between the cobbles carefully at every step. As he approached I even felt instinctively that he had been thinking much the same kind of thoughts as myself, then — frighteningly — that perhaps he would raise his face, and that under the brim of his hat I would find not merely someone I knew, but find myself, an exact, identical face and everything else. He was about the same height as I was, and seemed to be walking in much the same way (though of course he was working harder as he was climbing). We eventually came upon each other — I descending and he ascending — and halted face to face. He was sweating, but did not appear out of breath, as if afflicted with some recently contracted wasting disease that affected his temperature but not his breathing.

'Well hello there. We meet again,' he said.

'Indeed we do, but I really can't remember where it was that we met before.'

'Nor I,' he said, with a similar air of puzzlement.

'Well then, what is it that brings you up here?' I was really quite unhappy to be standing there conversing in this way with someone that I both knew and did not know. Of course, the climber felt likewise, and had considerable difficulty formulating an answer as his mind was apparently running over a long list of meetings and conventions at which we could possibly have met before.

'Ah, well it's business. Always business. It goes on and on and on. As soon as one thing is settled another one develops, doesn't it? But still, that's the way of the world. We'd be pretty unhappy if there was no business. All business is good business, isn't it? Or at least we are always busy, which is a good thing in itself.'

I asked him what kind of business he was in, hoping that this might provide a clue as to where we had met. His face, lined, cavernous, fitted something from my memory, and yet the link between the memory and the place or name was not to be had. Maybe we had met at some interministerial junket from the old days of the regency, or on a plane or train travelling to some conference or other.

'I am a bit of a master mariner,' he said. 'If you understand knots, or the knots that other people tie themselves in, then you might understand my business. I am really in the business of untying knots, unravelling problems. You might say I am a master mariner of human miseries.' He laughed drily and continued.

'Almost anything you care to mention: any ministry, department, section, bureau or subsection, any division, delegation, office or establishment is susceptible to my dexterities. Some of their knots are difficult to untie, but eventually an end is prised loose here or a loop is slipped out there, and then the whole thing falls away quickly, in a matter of seconds.'

For a moment I thought he was crazy, but he did not seem it. He was neither ragged and destitute, nor was he frightening and obviously deranged. In fact he was well dressed, polite and apparently rational, though this is not in itself proof of sanity.

'You see,' he carried on. 'I am the supplicant, or rather THE supplicant, because I am the only one. It is a dreadful isolated business and sometimes the sheer loneliness of it breaks me down completely and I lie awake in my hotel room with the curtains blowing in, my head full of bureau numbers, points of blackmail and appointments. I don't know what it is that drives me on, from one bureau to another, up and down the country. Of course the work is growing all the time, always expanding, always changing. Maybe I am looking for something that will defeat me totally. It becomes likely every year. You have no idea of the complexity of it all, the things one has to do to unearth an affidavit in triplicate from the basement of the Fisheries Department library in Ouled Street. Some days the smegma just envelopes me. After one has spent a whole afternoon on the terrace of the Café Voltaire disguised as a beggar, listening to the small talk of a drunken pen pusher, one begins to forget who one is altogether! Mind you that can be interesting too. In fact it is all interesting work. Ah yes, you have no idea how many new procedures they can come up with in a year. And then of course they don't necessarily stick to them, so there is always variety, and variety keeps the competition down. More than that; it is an escape from futility. Repetition is a constant reminder of futility my friend. Beware of repetition above everything else.'

The alley we were in seemed particularly gloomy, particularly enclosed, and his words had a certain wet sibillance to them, as if spoken by some creature that lived in dank rooms behind the streaming walls.

'So you sort out people's problems with the government?' I asked.

'Indeed I do, and a hard and wearing profession it is too, especially as one becomes old and the people one worked with — the contacts one has built up — retire and disappear and are replaced by new young faces of men who are keen, who truly believe that in the inking of their permit pads they are greasing the wheels of progress. Then I have to fill them with drink like their predecessors, and put them on their backs, to take a little bit of the enthusiasm out of their countersigning.' He seemed to become more gloomy.

'You know what I fear though? Do you really know what I fear? I fear above all the day the system becomes rational, when everyone can understand it. It will have neither mystery nor authority and people will not fear it. Above all, there will be no need for people like myself. I will be finished. Any idiot in a pair of running shorts will be able to work out how to get clearance for a pumping station, or a new water main, or a turnip patch, or whatever. And then, you know, I will really be conscious of it, really be conscious of a life that has been totally pissed up the wall!' He made an incongruous obscene gesture, entirely out of keeping with his suit and the polite way he had started upon the conversation. His hat was pulled down over his eyes, and I still could not conceive either of where I had encountered him, or why I had been singled out for this extraordinary lecture. The sun did not penetrate down into this particular alley, and the walls seemed to have moved in closer as we talked there on the steps, with our backs turned.

'I am sorry my friend,' he said, again becoming polite, urbane. 'I am sorry I have startled you. It is just that I thought I perceived some of the same anxieties in you that I have encountered and overcome in myself, and of course I could not let the opportunity slip.'

'What opportunity?'

'The opportunity to use what little knowledge I may have for the general benefit of supplicants everywhere. I see the beetling brow, the eyes obsessive and brooding, the tired step, and I think to myself, "Supplicant, here is another audience," and off I go.' He smiled lugubriously.

'Anyway, I can keep you no longer, you obviously have work to do, as we all have,' and with this he began to climb laboriously up the hill, until he turned down an alleyway that was so narrow that he was obliged to carry his briefcase over his head in order to enter it.

When he had disappeared from view I walked quickly until I came to the river at the heart of the old quarter, the very intestines of the city. The river tumbled down amongst the crooked houses. It was green in places, red or pink, as if full of the bile of the wasting generations piled in upon its banks. I fumbled in my pocket for Maria's letter, but pulled out only a slip of paper, rolled in a tube like a cigarette. MASTAGULATION it said.

I began hastily to climb back out of the deep ravine into which I had slipped leaving the tumbling gangrenous stream behind me. I passed the point where the supplicant had disappeared; then the streets became broader, the passers-by less ragged and less burdened, and soon the way led back out into the modern town, where neon signs flashed epileptically and boys on fast japanese scooters cut across the traffic, stealing handbags and racing through abandoned traffic lights.

In the early afternoon I came to the fountain in Boulevard du Pape, as Maria had instructed. It was easy to miss; the cherubs that had adorned the centre of the ornamental pond on which the fountain played had been broken off. The fountain itself was dry, and the retaining walls of its pool had been painted in red and white stripes and turned into a roundabout. Some enterprising citizens had let loose chickens in the pool where previously water had flowed, and they picked about in a desultory way amongst the litter that had blown in. The whole presented a mournful scene, though many people lounged against the wall in the sunlight, almost as if the fountain were still playing, as if they still heard it in their memories.

I had arrived early and felt conspicuous, felt as if everyone knew that I was looking for a girl. The people had that way of looking at you when you were doing this that indicated it was one of those things they did, but were careful enough to do discreetly. I walked around the fountain several times looking at faces, and several men approached me; 'Can I help you Monsieur? Change Money? Dirham, Dinar, Kopek? *Tu vas en Mauritanie? En Algerie? En France?*' I suppose as a European I should have been more purposeful, and swept past them with an angry grunt in a language they did not recognise. As it was they smiled and I smiled back, mumbling '*non . . . je veux pas,*' and acquired a following of money changers and lenders for minutes at a time. '*Je te donne un bon prix, Monsieur! Tu vas en Algerie, en Mauritanie?*' It was half past two by the painted clock over the plumber's shop at the corner of the square, and half past three by the clock on the post office, visible over the jumbled rooftops.

Then, eventually, I spotted her; she was walking fast with her head down, at a tangent to the edge of the pool. I caught up with her as she was leaving the square, but she hissed at me, and motioned me to follow at some distance. The afternoon was hot, and I followed her ten paces behind, keeping up with her short angry steps with difficulty. As we passed out of the cramped streets around the fountain I again had the impression that somehow things were closing in on her, half expected to turn and see some mediaeval figure with a knife clenched in his teeth shambling through the crowd, following her, following me.

However, soon we had turned into one of the main boulevards, where the crowds had a more cosmopolitan, impersonal air, and she slowed her pace so that I could catch up. When I was two or three paces behind she whispered at me, 'Where have you been? My God the men here are animals! I can't keep them off all the time. Why were you late?'

I came up behind her and noticed the same strong perfume that had been on the letter.

'It is already three. Well I suppose it's quite normal to be late.' She tossed her hair, then coughed nervously into a small white handkerchief with purple embroidered edges. She took my hand then, quite unexpectedly. Hers was surprisingly small, warm and smooth.

We looked in some shop windows at the various things that had come in from Europe for the rich people of the city. There were teddy bears and television sets with remote control, video recorders and casette players and dresses in the latest style from Paris. Then, in one shop there was nothing at all except a large illustrated book, sitting there in the window, on a kind of plinth. The lettering on the book had been lavishly picked out, developed into flowing scrolls and tumbling vine-tendrils. The girl stopped and looked at the book. 'It is the Koran,' she said. I had the feeling she was going to condemn it for a moment, but she pulled away from the window in silence.

'It's a beautiful book,' I said stupidly.

'Yes,' she said, and we went into a cramped baker's shop and bought some small flat cakes wrapped in thin paper. Later, we stopped to buy the latest edition of *Paris Match*, and she flicked over the pictures like an illiterate, then tossed the paper back to me. The shadows on the street were lengthening, acquiring that strange kind of mauve flavour that you can only see after you have been here a long time.

'I enjoyed your letter. Or at least I found it intriguing,' I said.

'Everyone finds me intriguing.'

'You said you were sad?'

'Maybe it's because I am lonely. I don't know. Look at those radio casettes.' Her attention had been caught by a great display of portable players, all chrome speakers and digital read-outs.

'But you cannot be lonely. I thought you were happy with your sister?'

'It makes me sad that they are all happy. My sister's husband has such a good job and the twins are perfect, or as perfect as boys can be.' Her high heels tapped along the pavement with discreet, deliberate steps. She gave the impression of very carefully controlled fury in almost everything she did, though other contradictory emotions seemed to be there too; the sudden softening in her tone, the immediate and transitory enthusiasms, the lines spoken with almost theatrical intensity.

'Did you mean what you said in the letter?'

'Of course I did. I'm not a liar, am I?' Then she laughed. 'When I first saw you l said to myself, "Maria, there is a man that you absolutely *must* have." I mean its not often one meets a handsome European, is it?' She had her face turned away again, and seemed to be awaiting my reply with some amusement. We passed the open doors of the Hotel Royale, and the smell of all really good hotels drifted out. Two flunkeys stood by the doors, fanning themselves with newspapers against the heat. An American couple were descending from a taxi; the husband white, bulging from cotton trousers, and the wife in a print dress with her face yellowed by too-frequent holidays in hot climates. They snapped at each other, in a pointless kind of way.

'You want that kind of thing?' she asked. 'Is that what you Europeans aim for, to be gross like that, with a fat white wife with bad veins and a mind full of suet; old and wrinkled like a baked potato, a great paunchy sweat bag of a woman? You'll end up with her you know Narrator.'

We turned up a side street for no particular reason.

'Tell me, what is it that you want Narrator?' she asked.

But we were already on the steps of the hotel, its ill-painted doors held back by a leather catch-strap that was hooked against the wall of the hallway. There were no flunkeys here, and I could feel her body against me, her hand up under my shirt, my own perspiration between her fingers. The boy on the counter in the lobby blinked expressionlessly while blue-bottles circled almost invisibly in the cool gloom above. Somewhere out the back, someone was frying vegetables. I signed the register absurdly as Mr. and Mrs. Smith. As we climbed the stairs, the heavy key clanking in my hand, I could hear an Arab tape playing, repeating the same phrase over and over again, maybe a love song. In fact definitely a love song, as there was nothing else.

Up under the roof it was hot and the carpets were thread-bare. The girl walked in front of me slowly, her hips swaying. As we unlocked the door, my hands slipped up under her shirt and over the smooth slippery brown skin. Then a curious violence came over us both, with the sleazy room, the circumstances; she unzipped me and drew me out. The curtains were too long, trailing across the floor. I caught a brief glimpse of her sex, then her mouth closed in on me, her tongue lapped me. I threw her on the bed and entered her. We drove into each other, more and more violently, in a kind of awful dry empty fury, then fell from the bed and I slipped out of her. She crawled towards me and I plunged into her again, but this time she cried out in Arabic and gripped herself around me and I began to fuck her to somehow stop it all, but again slipped out and then exploded up and out all over her clothes, in one great fountain. But she had not finished, because her hands, her fingers worked across her sex; she moaned as if in the most awful agony imaginable, until finally she let out a wild empty cry and went suddenly limp. Then she rolled over and began crying in a kind of mournful, lost sort of way. Her shoulders shook gently, the floor of the room was dusty, and some of it clung to my knees. There was a faint smell of boiled cabbage and cats. Various items of clothing lay discarded at random. My shirt had its buttons torn off. Her back was bleeding where my watch strap had cut across it.

'*Laisse-moi. Tu veux?*' She asked.

I stood looking at her, somehow not wanting to touch her at all, and yet wanting to comfort her in some way.

'Please leave me now,' she said again, but still I stood there.

'Narrator, *please!*' Slowly I began to dress, while she lay there quite still, as she had done on Murphy's bed, the faint whisper of her breathing barely audible, as if waiting for it to start again. I opened the door and looked back into the darkened room, but there was no response, no movement. I went out, closing the door softly, listened for a moment, but there was still silence within. It was then that I remembered something that I had noticed in our coupling; she had had steel teeth, a complete set, silver, perfect, but made of steel.

At seven that evening I stepped out of a taxi in the suburbs. The driver had taken me by circuitous routes to the gates of Sbiti's club, and I stood upon the road under the plane trees which canopied the iron gates and threw black–green shadows amongst the hedgerows. Somewhere tennis balls were being knocked back and forth, because in the evening air I could hear the grunts that preceded fast services, and the sound of gym shoes running for distant lobbed balls.

The gates of the club were guarded by an imbecile in torn shorts, wearing a striped jumper and barefoot. He was perched on a stool by the gate (in fact all iron gates in the city tended to have people perched on stools beside them). I pressed my face between the bars of the gate.

'I have come to see Monsieur Sbiti.'

The guardian of the gates rose with the bewildered slowness of such people, and began searching in his pockets, abstractedly, for the keys to the gate. There were three of them, each one tied to his belt by a different coloured piece of string. The colours might have been a code to tell him which of the locks they were destined for, but the imbecile appeared to have forgotten which one was which. Laboriously he tried one key after another, murmuring Sbiti's name as he did so.

Eventually the gates opened and he asked me who I wished to see, although I had only just told him moments before.

'*Ah, oui . . . Monsieur Sbiti . . . Sbiti? . . . Sbiti,*' he said, waving his arms up the path towards the clubhouse to indicate the direction I should take.

I strolled towards the sound of tennis, across the gravel swept into patterns by the gardeners; the borders of the path were planted with European flowers, kept alive by the continuous watering. I could see thick red hosepipes gurgling in the undergrowth, see the earth unusually black where it had been freshly watered and weeded. I came to the clubhouse, a long white wooden building with a slatted verandah overlooking the tennis courts. Palm trees overhung the wicker chairs that were laid out on the patio to complete the complex parody of some imaginary colonial past. As I came nearer, however, I realised that the general impression was marred by a pile of damaged chairs that seemed to have been left to await collection or disposal in the middle of the space between clubhouse and tennis courts, where they had since developed a conspicuous patina of green mould.

On the balcony too, things were not as might have been expected, because the drinkers and sportsmen were clothed in a bizarre mélange of different garments, with the ubiquitous unmatching tracksuit predominant amongst djellabas and T Shirts from America and Taiwan. Some slumped, obviously exhausted, in brief swimming costumes, and drank largely from tall glasses decorated with sprigs of mint or some other local herb. For a moment I closed my eyes, maybe in an attempt to capture some fantastical dream-moment, in which the murmur of the foreign voices, the smell of the cut grass and continental tobacco would all come together, but it all seemed to slip past me; the words barely audible, the smells as if sealed behind plate glass, the atmosphere discordant with the desired form of that elusive dream. My mind was somehow overburdened, bunged full of all kinds of thoughts; tired, wasted to the extent that it had not the time to handle even the simplest of social niceties.

I approached Sbiti where I had spotted him, in the corner where he could watch the girls working in the kitchens, surrounded by friends or confidants. He was laughing and had a big glass of Algerian Ricard on the table in front of him, with his feet pushed into yellow slippers. His T shirt incongruously advertised that it was 'The Property of HM Prison, Brixton', and clashed with his green running shorts.

'*Aaah, Monsieur Narrator, quel plaisir . . .*' he cried, getting up and fetching a chair for me, apparently delighted that I had come. Ostentatiously, he clicked his fingers for the waiter and shouted at him before he was even half way across the floor: '*Un whisky pour le Monsieur!*' Then he introduced me to the assembled company.

'Gentlemen', we have a great honour that Monsieur Narrator, a great friend from our ally the Kingdom of England, should have seen fit to come here to do business with us tonight.' He spoke loudly, and managed to silence conversation at the table both behind us and in front of us.

'This is Monsieur Mechbar, a surgeon at the Royal Infirmary, and this is Monsieur Pernod, the director of the bureau of elections. Over here we have Mohammed the dentist, and Mustafa the head of the faculty of science.' We shook hands and smiled.

'You see,' continued Sbiti. 'It is not only in Europe that we have the good things of this life.' He waved his arms expansively to take it all in, and I agreed that it was good to see such a place, and answered a few polite questions about my work. The director of the bureau of elections laughed enormously at almost everything that was said. At one point he knocked the entire contents of his glass over into the ashtray, creating a soup of cigarette ends which he then threated to pour over Sbiti's head. However, the waiter appeared obligingly and carried the mess away into the inner recesses of the building with some quick aside that amused election man greatly. Sbiti laughed too, and slapped Monsieur Election roundly on the back, so you could hear his hollow chest. Of course it was all a little pretentious, but yet a pretension without any great air of success, as if those indulging in drink and tennis were quietly mocking the habits of their European neighbours. I sensed a certain bitterness about it all.

As Monsieur Election (as they began to call him) became more drunk, they filled his glass up with increasingly terrifying measures of alcohol. They propped him up in his chair as he slipped down; then he would slip again, and they would gather round and heave him up by the armpits, and he would smile myopically, start to think, then smile mournfully and commence his descent again. We were talking about trade, and Sbiti was expanding on his explanation for the difficulties in the economy at the time.

'You see, I know it is all highly technical, but the credits we use to buy abroad are all fixed for us by our bankers in New York,' he explained.

'Aaaaagh. New York,' muttered Monsieur Election, struggling vaguely in the depths of his chair.

'Liza Minelli ... the subway ... am I not right Monsieur Narrator?'

'Yes, yes, absolutely,' we all said. Sbiti carried on.

'Now the exports of tomatoes are *crucial*.'

'The tomato, now there's a thing ...,' said Monsieur Election.

'...And the tomato is very much influenced by the climate, so there are times that we find the demand of our clients in Amsterdam and Brussels difficult to satisfy. You cannot imagine the extent to which your European salad is dependent on your African tomato.'

'...*Exacte* ... *exacTEMENT!* ...' burbled Monsieur Election.

The doctor added some thoughts on diet, the scientist mentioned some research he had heard of on the aubergine in a hot climate, the conversation went back and forth; the ministry's policy was mentioned, but not explained. Soon it became late and guests began to make their way out along the gravel paths, now floodlit, with their tennis rackets and sports bags. Monsieur Election had let his head slide onto the table and was rocking it gently from side to side, mumbling, now almost entirely incoherent. I tried to bring the conversation around to my business, but it would not respond. Like a large class in school following a wasp that has come through the window, the figures in the circle were continually distracted and could not be brought to the point. I paid various extensive bills (the prices naturally inflated to keep out a certain class of person), and repeatedly tried to slip my pump-house deal into the dialogue, but found myself humiliated again and again by the way it was ignored with great good humour. Eventually, angered by some facile remark from the dentist, I leant forward and whispered in Sbiti's ear that we had to come to the point, that my time was not only limited, but valuable. His eyes were bright and spittle hung from the corner of his mouth. His hands worked vaguely over a packet of cigarettes. Then he put his arm around me affectionately.

'Aaah. Do not worry. Above all do not worry. Worry is a dreadful thing. Everything will be fine as it always is. Who knows? Maybe you lose this little business of yours, but there are always other businesses, are there not? That is the way with business. Even if there are not, you are always fine, in yourself, as a man. You can go away when you like and go to England or anywhere else; you people are always all right, no matter what. Am I not right?' The doctor detected Sbiti's sharpness of tone and placed a gentle hand on his jacket sleeve.

'He is . . . a good man,' he said. 'We are all good men. If my friend Monsieur Sbiti can help you he will, and if he cannot he will not. Please, monsieur, do not press him on this matter.'

'FUCK BUSINESS,' said Monsieur Election suddenly from the tabletop, stopping the whole conversation. For a moment we were all uncertain if he had really spoken; his head still lay upon the table, motionless in the gloom. Then he seemed to lift himself up, as if by an enormous effort of drunken will.

'He is a little tired,' said the doctor.

'Tired,' said Monsieur Election, half in agreement, or perhaps considering whether it was a true description of his condition. Sbiti began to put away his tennis equipment hurriedly, watching Monsieur Election all the time.

'Yesh. Always tired. It's natural,' said Monsieur Election, apparently gathering steam for some large pronouncement.

'Give me your address,' said Sbiti, rolling his gym shoes in his towel and tucking them under his arm.

'Quickly, before things become unpleasant. I will see what I can do. If I can do anything, I will. I am most sorry about my friend. Maybe we can arrange a meeting with Zoboti.' He seemed to have changed his mind, to now be considering the whole issue merely because I had lost interest in it, a matter of pride perhaps.

'ZOBOTI. ... BASTARD! ... BASTARD! ... BASTARD!' shouted Monsieur Election at the top of his voice, like a cheer leader on some huge demonstration, like a demonstration of one, and the voice echoed back from the empty plate glass of the dining room and the select bar, freezing every remaining face at the outside tables.

'BASTARD! ... BASTARD! ... BASTARD! ...' he cried, over and over.

I could see that tears streamed down his face. Then he stopped and began weeping quite openly, and the waiter came up, frightened, confused that a social superior should have got so dangerously out of control. Sbiti seemed on the point of physically forcing his towel down Monsieur Election's throat, and yet could not bring himself to do it.

'Driss, Driss! Stop it.' he said, pulling at his face with his hands to stop the noise coming out. Sbiti slipped a note into the waiter's palm, and made small disappearing gestures to him, and then, when this failed to move him, he pulled out an even larger note and whispered some brief, discreet instructions.

Monsieur Election was by now murmuring '99 percent ... 99 percent ...' for some reason, interspersed with tears.

'Abdullah will see to him,' said Sbiti, moving away, encouraging us to follow, fearful of some new and seriously incriminating outburst from his friend.

'*Quel Salaud! On ne peut pas croire ça. Quel dégoutant*,' he said, for the benefit of the few remaining drinkers.

Despite this I have no doubt that our departure appeared ragged, a defeat of sorts, a disgrace for Sbiti. In the floodlights the flowers now seemed discoloured, all yellow-blues and luminous greens. Sbiti apologised in an almost automatic monologue as the imbecile, still wide-awake, struggled with the keys to the wrought-iron gate.

'I cannot understand it,' said Sbiti. His friends agreed, wiping condensation from their new cars, fallen leaves from the windscreens. 'I really cannot understand it. A man of the utmost probity,' and so on.

Sbiti drove me back to my hotel erratically. The city at that hour of the morning had been swept clean of people, so the waves of litter that blew along the main boulevards were more clearly visible. The pavements were brightly lit, and odd deformed cats and dogs roamed there amongst the garbage left out by the restaurants and the European stores. Congregations of tabbies scrabbled around, overturning bins, chasing rats, like any other city. Sbiti seemed pre-occupied now, and we skidded around some roundabouts, past the point where I had met Maria, now totally empty and quite desolate. Twice we were stopped by patrols, looming out from the damp streets unexpectedly, but were swiftly waved through when Sbiti flashed his ministry card.

'Maybe one day I will have a ministry car,' he said. 'Red number plates. No stopping.' Then he slipped back into silence.

He left me at the door of my hotel, or as near to it as he could manage. He seemed tired, somehow discouraged, dishevelled in a way that I had often seen. He left his engine running while I thanked him for the evening. He again hoped that I had not been offended by Monsieur Election's behaviour. It was unforgiveable, he said. As I closed the door of his big Mercedes, I laughed and said that I wondered if Zoboti would ever get to hear about the scene at the club.

'I mean it doesn't matter to me. That's why you can relax. But of course, you cannot be sure that I have your interests at heart while there are outstanding problems. You see, Monsieur Sbiti, business goes on like you say.' I smiled and slammed the door before he could reply, his face surprised behind the glass, imprisoned in his Mercedes. You see, a certain amount of clarity was required, some organising principle.

I stumbled up the lino'd steps to my room, everything jaundiced by the shadeless bulbs over the stairs, and then stopped outside the door. The light was on inside. Repair Man was there, in bed, reading a newspaper or perhaps just dreaming, planning, awake, active. I could not take that; I had finished with it all for the day and yet I had to sleep, if I could: had to rest, to stop, anywhere. I entered the room, which was brightly lit, almost cosy, and felt as if Repair Man had lived in it all his life. The newspaper was laid face down on the bed where he had finished reading, and he looked fixedly at the mantelpiece, where the clock now stood; just the mechanism, not the case. It was working now, the pendulum swung back and forth, and a slow regular tick filled the room. The hand showed the correct time, though as yet the face had not been fixed in place.

'Hello, Repair Man,' I said stupidly. With the bright light, the clock ticking, the newspaper, I felt somehow defective, dishonest. I undressed, but still he did not speak, it was as if there were something religious in his disapproval, in the calm intensity of it. He would not strike out to show how he felt, but would just sit there calmly disapproving. That was what religion was about; nothing you could really hate. He had that fatal look on him, like the really hard teachers at school who always had perfect order. I climbed into bed, but could not even begin to sleep. I thought of Maria, crudely, overtly, but the light seemed to penetrate even these thoughts, and even when it was turned off I could sense that he was not lying down to rest, but was picking my mind apart, weighing the lousy imperfections of my every action.

The next morning I was awake before him, because I was awake all night, had heard the wailing mosque at one and again at four, had heard the last and the first cock crow, the sounds of the milk coming into the kitchen, and the night porter with some whore in the reception, so much so that I felt I had finally heard even the secret breathing of the place, its last ghastly surreptitious nighttime breath.

I changed my hotel, moving across to the Metropole, down by the river. I left a note for the hotel keeper for my mail to be forwarded, and paid the bill. I also left instructions that Repair Man should not be told of my whereabouts. I paid his bill as well, but then even at the end of things, there are obligations I suppose.

TUESDAY 7TH OCTOBER

I slept late in my new hotel, though at first I had had difficulty falling asleep at all; the sheets had stuck to me, become
damp with sweat, then prickly, as if a plateful of bread
crumbs had been emptied into the bed. Then I had dozed
vaguely, and the events, the ingredients of the previous day
had brewed up in my mind to form a kind of awful stew,
through which characters and events floated in surprising
juxtaposition; at one point mother was there, her fingers
massaging Maria's nipples, and then Repair Man with them
both in some lewd combination which they had tried to
disguise from me by hiding behind a pink curtain, and by
shouting the most transparent excuses across to where I stood
on the other side.

However, as the first grey light of the Tuesday morning
seeped around the shutters, I had fallen into a profound and
heavy sleep, a sleep of the most total black emptiness that I
think I have ever encountered. When I awoke I could not
even begin to lift my head from the embroidery of the pillow-
slip, but lay looking through slits of gummed-up eyes at the
needlework. 'Hotel Metropole' it said, and whoever had sewn
the name had started their work with Gothic script and then
abandoned it halfway through and reverted to capitals. I lay
there, considering why this might be for quite some time,
and then became anxious about whether I would in fact ever
be fully awake again. My body seemed unable to obey any
of my commands: I could not make the slightest movement.
Somewhere outside heavy traffic was moving along hot, dusty
roads, and the muffled cries of the maids could be discerned
in the corridors, changing the linen and singing to each other.
It was curiously restful now to lie there suspended away from
it all, half asleep, to hear the running of showers, the distant
moaning of hoovers and vacuum cleaners.

A thick bar of sunlight, so powerful as to appear almost
solid, burnt across the red and green blanket on my bed, and

up the mauve wallpaper to the ceiling, so it was already late morning, perhaps even midday.

When finally I levered myself out of bed I felt elated, light-hearted, and drew back the curtains on one of those perfectly blue clear days, one of those days that can pick out the special colours in the most uninspiring scene, the ochre in the brickwork of tenements, or the ebony in chimney soot. In my underpants, I ventured out onto the balcony, where a faint breeze licked along past my sixth floor window. Looking down, I could see small figures scuttling along the pavement underneath, and on a balcony below mine a family were at lunch, served by a waiter in a white jacket. They had set a radio on the stone balustrade, and the noise of a French pop station floated up. '*Et voilá, c'est Martine Napoléon avec sa nouvelle chanson . . . Merci, Martine.*' The presenter burbled irrepressibly out into the sunlit morning, while the knives and forks clinked solidly on the heavy, expensive dinner plates.

Later, I picked my way downstairs past the mounds of laundry that the maids had deposited on every landing, down to the entrance hall where the day porter was reading *Le Matin du Sahara* and eating a boiled egg. From time to time, he dipped the egg in a small twist of spice that he had propped carefully between his velvet uniformed knees. As I went past him he shouted out:

'Hey, Monsieur, you sleep too well? Wait one moment, I have some urgent letters for you. You are an important man, I think, to have all these messengers running after you.'

I signed for the letters and showed my identity card (though he knew quite well who I was). One of the letters was in a vellum envelope, with the King's stamp on it in red wax, with *par main . . . urgence* typed under my address. The second was obviously from Maria, and identical with the one I had received the day before. A third letter was there too, some circular from one of the English firms I dealt with from time to time. It had been sent on by Murphy; I recognised his handwriting and the way it had been somehow scrumpled and abraded, as if carried in his back pocket for a period of days, before he had remembered to post it on to me. I thanked the porter, and he grinned.

'Letters from beautiful girls, letters from the King, letters from Europe, *that* is the way to start the day!' He patted my arm with disturbing familiarity, as if he had already read my letters and somehow knew enough about me to make these gestures. However, the envelopes showed no signs of tampering.

'All it takes is intelligence,' said the porter, and patted my arm again in the same way.

I chose one of the cafés up near the ministry, one of the seats which I had envied in my walk to meet Sbiti. It was one of those café terraces where everything sparkled in white or glass or crystal-gilt, where almost every surface reflected some aspect of oneself or one's friends, a café of ultimate vanity. I ordered a beer, and settled to read my post, starting with the least interesting and working upwards, according to a schedule I had developed years before.

The letter from England was some publicity blurb from a firm in the North.

'Dear Mr. Narrator,' it began, in that personalised way that computers now seem able to manage. 'Herewith details of our latest product. As you can see this replaces the swivel mounted transverse pinion trunnel ... the small buttock-piece has been gorbellied to allow a freer lateral action with consequent savings in drift ... the nipple connecting the bladder valve to the horizontal down-pipe has been margin-ally gimped to facilitate easy greasing-up ... through suction-quotients are merely tentative ... thorough manipulation ensures a steady flow under *even the most arduous tropical conditions.*'

I crumpled this nonsense up and threw it away. I couldn't remember what the original product was that this one had replaced, but knew that I would never find anyone that would have wanted it, or would even consider its successor.

The next letter, from the ministry — from where I sat I could see the white economy-rococo facade — was really a major step forward. It was from Sbiti, indeed from a now frightened Sbiti, or more frightened than he had been before.

It was on official paper, with the full title of the ministry occupying the top quarter of the page, with the names of the various secretaries and under-secretaries crammed in underneath in Arabic and French. Some of these names had been crossed out clumsily in red ink. The message was brief, though maybe that was the intention behind the overgrown letterheading.

Dear Monsieur Narrator,

I have the honour of advising you that M. Zoboti will receive you tomorrow morning at 10 AM. He has asked me to inform you that you should bring all the relevant documents and papers, and *restrict your discussion only to those immediate matters in hand at this particular moment in time.*

Veuillez agréer, Monsieur, l'expression de mes sentiments distinguées.

Mohammed Sbiti.

My mood of optimism heightened, and I ordered another beer, opening Maria's letter as the waiter returned. The perfume I found brought with it an aching, physical sensation. There was the same crabbed, cramped handwriting and the scalloped edges to the pages and an odd indefinable guilt about my manner as I read.

Dear Narrator,

My body aches with yearning and I find I cannot sleep now at all, that I long for you all the time, to be with you, to have you take me as before . . . I know I should not, but then this increases my longing, my emptiness, my desire, until I excite myself even in writing this. You cannot imagine how terrible the boredom is here, the way in which the shadows close in upon me. Oh Narrator, please meet me again at the fountain on Boulevard du Pape, and we can make love again. Meet me today, at 2 PM.

Yours for ever, Maria

P.S. Destroy this letter totally, except in your memory.

I laughed, and drank down the froth on my beer, congratulating myself on the days general good fortune. I read the letter again, and it began to excite me, in a crude and unromantic kind of way, and as it excited me it blinded me, almost as the sunlight did, reflecting back from the mirrors and cut glass, reflecting back upon my judgement. I paid the waiter, hailed a taxi and grinned stupidly at myself in the driver's mirror, the words in the letter ludicrous but titillating, appropriate to the exact moment of that particular day.

However, as the taxi manoeuvred through the traffic, closer to the dry fountain (at times its striped edges could be seen down side streets), a certain shyness began to come on me, as if the very explicitness of my intentions made them visible to everyone, as if somehow I were exploiting the girl, or (and this was a deeper, less clearly perceived anxiety) that she was in some way exploiting me. I could not as yet think in what way that might be, what it was that she was taking from me, what was the purpose of this exercise in romantic perversity? And of course that too drew me on, and yet frustrated me in a way that added that particular violence to our meetings, that particular disjunction in everything we said and did together.

Thus, when I finally stepped down and paid off the taxi driver in crumpled notes, there was a slight reserve in the way I approached her, sitting there on a stone bench with her back to the dry fountain. She was reading a book, and two mongrel dogs fought each other in a pool behind her, provoked by a group of youths who threw stones at them. There was a silence at first, apart from the noise of the dogs barking and then she stood up and kissed me briefly on the cheek. Then she sat down and turned the book over in her lap so that I could not see what she had been reading.

'You received my letter?' She whispered the words, apparently embarrassed. People passed in the street, looking at us curiously. 'Did you like it?'

'I did.'

All my earlier excitement had gone. I noticed she was dressed again in the tight jeans she had had when I first met her, the high heels, the thin cotton shirt, but that these things had no effect on me.

There was now another silence, and the two dogs skulked away in different directions.

'Tiens,' she said 'I have bought you something.' From her bag she pulled a brown paper parcel and unwrapped it with deliberation, as if the object inside could be easily damaged and neither replaced nor repaired. The parcel contained a grey lambswool sweater with a V-neck, one that was absurdly like my old school pullover, yet much more expensive.

'It was made in England. Look at the label.' I looked; the pullover had been made by some firm off St James's in London.

'Do you like it? It will make you very smart, very much the businessman for the winter.' I thanked her for it, but she said:

'Oh, I don't need your thanks. It's nothing anyway. Put it away and we'll go for a walk. I do not like sitting here,' and she was on her feet before we could discuss the matter. She put the book away in her bag carefully, and I glimpsed the title, *Contes d'Amour*, and the cover showing one of those badly drawn couples; the girl with windswept hair and big eyes, the man with the angular face and devouring look, holding the girl's forearm.

'So you read romantic fiction?'

'From time to time. A friend lent it to me.'

'What else do you read?'

'Oh, this and that.'

We walked, and I tried to engage in conversation, but all our talk seemed to founder on some mutual misapprehension, or at some point where she would become short with me and refuse to say more.

'Have you had any news of your family?'

'I had a letter from my mother. She is unhappy with the worry of the farm while my father is away.'

'I didn't know you had a farm. I thought your father was in business.'

'I told you. You haven't forgotten?'

'Where is the farm? Is it a large one?'

'Oh yes, it's quite large; we keep horses you know. I love riding in the spring.'

'Do you go hunting there?'

'What is hunting?'

I explained to her.

'It seems stupid to me, stupid and cruel, but I suppose that kind of thing gives you pleasure,' she said.

And so it went on. She seemed in fear of her father, and when I went further she would snap back at me that he was part of her family, and that I was not to take him away. Her mother knitted a lot and she studied geology. She found it boring.

'*Enfin*, most things are boring,' she said, and daintily kicked an empty yoghurt carton off the pavement into the gutter.

'But you have opportunities.'

'Huh.'

I noticed that we had come again upon the street where the hotel was, in fact had willed that we would. I did not argue with her because otherwise I knew we would not come there, and she provoked me, maybe to see how much I would take. At any rate, when we reached the door, our pace slowed, we talked of nothing, at cross purposes.

Then she said:

'*Écoute, je suis fatigué*. I want to sleep,' a sudden reminder — none too oblique — that the same thought that was in my mind had been circulating in hers, that it was not all some dream, some fantasy.

The desk-clerk handed us the keys again, and I felt the same vague shame I had felt earlier, only stronger. Oddly, the lighting, dingy and flickering, gave her complexion the pallor of a sick child, and a dread that I would not be able to perform came upon me. The hotel seemed more musty than before, the carpets more threadbare; since our last visit one whole section had been rolled up and lay the length of one of the unused corridors. An old picture of the King hung askew on the second floor landing, with rouged lips, observing our progress. She climbed up ahead of me, her behind swaying, with an easy sense of familiarity, a subtle, sensual ease in the the way she had taken the hotel keys from my hand, between her long painted nails, and in the way she encouraged me to help her with the door. I found myself seeking something in her which would excite rather than make me anxious, and as I sought my anxiety grew. I thought as we entered the room that maybe she had brought me there to humiliate me.

"I don't know you Maria. We can't really go on,' I said.

She turned around, unbuttoned her shirt and dropped it on the floor. She raised her hands over her head and clasped them together, back to front, like a ballet dancer, and yawned widely.

'Surely it doesn't matter. I mean no one knows anyone, do they?'

She unclipped her brassière, quite slowly.

'I mean you should not be so sad, so serious about these matters.'

'I can't help it, I mean it is all so baffling.'

'That is maybe why I like you then, because you cannot help it; being sad I mean. People who cannot help themselves are far more likeable than people who can.' She sat on the bed, and bent down to unbuckle her shoes. She had delicate feet. I began to undress, watching her and she watching me, but still I was not at ease; there was a calculation going on somewhere and I could not establish what it was about.

'Can you help me,' she said. She wore a tiny slip and I moved towards her and she began to suck me, gently, drawing me out, and then suddenly I had the desire to humiliate her in turn, to somehow force her to reveal something other than her body to me. I pressed her on to me, holding her there, but she continued sucking, her lips worked on me, I could feel her tongue, her fingers clenched in my buttocks. I let her move as she wished, and she stood up, kissing me hard on the mouth and running her hands over my penis. Then a frenzy overtook me, with her stockinged thighs slipping on my back, the endless warm thrusting of her sex, her nipples against my chest, diving into her, driving on and on and on, as she shouted obscenities. We fought, ground against each other, but still somehow neither would release to the other, as if some third person were there between us, inhibiting complete satisfaction. Finally, she wriggled from under me, took my organ again in her mouth, and began a rythmic lapping motion, faster and faster until I burst into her mouth, through whatever barrier it was that had divided me from her. I held her to me again but she struggled free and rushed to the sink, where she began washing her mouth quite urgently, almost desperately, as if expecting to choke at any moment on my juices. When she had finished, she began to put on her clothes almost immediately, as if I had angered her in someway. I tried to help her, but she pushed me away.

'*Tu es un salopard,*' she said. '*Il ne faut jamais faire ça avec une fille!*'

When she was dressed however, she seemed to draw herself together, to somehow re-organise her reactions, and she came across to me, and briefly cradled my head against her breast, even made herself kiss me. But I could tell some law of sexual etiquette had come between us, or at any rate that is what I assumed.

'*Salut*, Narrator. Tomorrow I will see you again,' she said, picked up her bag and strode the few feet across to the door, as if only minutes remained before the departure of a train that would take her away, clear away from the room and me and everything I represented in her mind. It was as if the whole episode had had a fixed time limit, as if all our conversation had been unnecessary. The door slammed and I called after her, but her footsteps, precise and definite, faded away along the corridor, then down the stairs.

I was still kneeling on the bed half-clothed where she had left me. I felt cold and I could smell my own sweat, already becoming stale upon my skin. Her saliva down there irritated me too, and I went to the sink and washed myself carefully, then dressed, with increasing speed, pulled open the door and threw myself down the stairs and out into the darkening evening street after her. I looked left and right and tried to see into a tram that had just pulled away, but Maria had already vanished. I ran through the crowds, pushing my way ahead, somehow enraged by the whole affair, and caught a fleeting glimpse of her as I reached the first corner. Then, having run to that corner I found myself only a few yards behind her, as she had stopped to buy a copy of *Le Matin du Sahara*. She began walking again; the same precise, self-contained steps, the bag with the romantic novel swinging at her side. I was sweating again, my legs felt flabby, weak; I felt suddenly sick and exhausted and began to follow her at some distance, doggedly, with no real hope of it ever resolving anything, now no longer anxious to confront her. In fact the more I followed those steady steps of hers, the more aware I became that I had nothing to confront her with in any case.

She continued walking, until we passed right out of the central area of the city, into the more seedy neighbourhoods where there were no pavements, where the cafés became more and more derelict, and the people sat without buying. Finally even the tram line stopped, but still she walked until the skyline turned a deeper shade of orange, and she turned down an alley with a quick glance to left and right, like some small animal preparing for sleep. I ran to the corner, but already she had gone as I knew she would. The street was made of mud and some ragged children played in the water that lay there from a burst main, the water briefly burnished by the last stray beams of evening sunlight. A group of men were stripping parts from a rusting Mercedes dumped cross-ways in the middle of the road, its bonnet stoved in by some accident. I was half tempted to ask them if they had seen her or where she had gone, but a sudden sense of futility overcame me. I retraced my steps as the last business conversations of the day buzzed in the telephone lines overhead.

Back at my hotel I found a large buff envelope had been deposited in my room, by my bedside table, and I tore it open carelessly, believing it to be some new drawings I had been expecting from England, prepared to toss them down if they were. Instead I found a manuscript from Murphy, with a brief typed note attached to it. 'HOPE YOU LIKE IT. SEE YOU SOON'. I was about to drop it on the floor when the first line arrested my attention.

'The businessman liked foreign girls, and a thin drool of saliva escaped his lips as he unzipped his trousers. Foreign girls made him forget all the other old humiliations. But when Maria looked at him, she could barely hide her contempt, though she had to, for he represented things she wanted, with his white bulging stomach sprayed with ginger hairs, his awful unwashed smell, his black plastic wallet, above all with his passport, his sheer nationality. He was foreign; he could get her away. But he smelt bad, and one hand scratched through the ginger hair as he looked at her with fascination — at her breasts, not her face — at her body, not her expression. It was a dreadful empty kind of fascination he had, a sort of temporary, loveless hunger.'

I read on with increasing horror, realising that Murphy in some way was describing events that were painfully recent, and personal to myself and the girl, or at least I had hoped that they were personal in that way. I could not think how it came to be written, and hoped in some way it was pure invention, a pure fiction. Yet as I read on, the things that we had done: the noises, the cries, the gestures, were mostly all there, tricked out in Murphy's bad prose. Some parts, in fact most parts of the text, tallied almost exactly with what we had done, though the room was different (a hunting scene in greenish watercolour hung on the walls for example). The steel teeth could not have been ignored by Murphy; in fact he would have used them unpleasantly, in some kind of special way. The man had a large mole just above his navel and I had not, and I did not have a plastic wallet at all. Above all, and quite crucially, I was not the kind of man that he had described; it was not even a plausible parody of myself. And yet, he had known her, there was a chance that he still did know her. He could be dredging in the past for things that he had done with her, but that still did not account for his sending me this sordid manuscript.

'When he had finished taking her from behind (though she had tried to turn him desperately), he patted her buttocks with his porcine fingers. There was dirt under the fingernails. His eyes took her in, swallowed her for some future reference on lonely nights when there were no other girls to be had. He coughed, and spat on his handkerchief, one more little job done.'

I read through the text carefully, underlining the sections that could apply to me, and leaving the rest clear of marks. Halfway through the text it became apparent that this dismal exercise would reveal no clear answer; some sections, not too many, were underlined and others were not. Even the sections I thought related to me could easily apply to someone else, and there was ultimately no clear conclusion except that the girl was Maria. There are certain intimate details that even weak powers of description cannot obfuscate.

The uncertainty (on top of other uncertainties) became annoying, enraging. I drank a glass of water from the tap, then spat the rest out, as it was warm and soapy, with a faint tang of disinfectant. The girl was undoubtedly Maria and yet she could not have done the things that she had, responded in the way that she had. . . . There was something in the text that was false; a desire to shock, without the necessary attention to emotional detail.

On the other hand, I remembered her hurried washing, the quick steps, as if she had been disgusted with herself, unwilling to pay me even the most cursory attentions. Maybe she had gone straight back to Murphy, to some low ceilinged room, to have him smoke and ask her about the very inside details of the whole affair. There was, in fact, no conceivable way of looking at it that was satisfactory from the point of view of any of us, and I took the text and tore it up into small pieces, before throwing it in the bin (why do hotel keepers always assume people will be tearing things up and throwing them away?)

It was only after a period of staring at the ceiling, with my feelings somehow locked within me, that I came to one final plausible solution that would allow me to sleep. Perhaps

Murphy had written it unaware that I had met the girl and with some other person in mind as the central character. Perhaps it was another coincidence, another unfortunate juxtaposition, and he had not intended to shock or humiliate me at all.

WEDNESDAY 8TH OCTOBER

When I awoke, the events of the previous day seemed to have re-organised themselves into a new and more pleasing perspective, as if sleep had given me the necessary resources to fix upon the least damaging interpretations, and then to file them away at the back of my mind. The shredded paper in the basket was now there more as a reminder of some momentary grand unpleasantness, rather than as a stimulant to further depressing thoughts. Nonetheless I rang down for the maid, and had it swiftly removed, after ensuring that the text had truly been torn into fragments too tiny for anyone to read.

When this was done, I opened the shutters on another fine day. The warm morning air blew in from the balcony, a perfect breeze. Had I ever really believed that my activities here were any different from anyone else's? One always does, but then perhaps that is merely vanity. Munton, in one of his less sober moments had once slurred something to me about 'the logic of loneliness', when I had first arrived. Maybe that was all it was with the girl. Funnily enough, Munton had withdrawn the remark immediately he saw that I had understood it, but then I suppose that is fairly typical too. Anyway, what did it matter? Maria and Murphy could well be out there, but my desire to meet them, to communicate with them in any way had gone. They could well be out there together, down some alley strung with washing and television antennae and debris, but the alleys were a complex network and my chances of meeting either were considerably lengthened by the geography of the place. I would see Murphy back in Goughly, by which time it would have faded anyway. He'd probably have proof that he'd never been in the capital at all.

So it was that after breakfast I again made my way up towards the ministry, to keep my appointment with Zoboti; not in good humour, but more cheerfully than I might have expected the previous evening. I drifted up along the pavements, past the same progressive luxuriance in the cafés, and up to the same gates I had passed through with Repair Man on our first visit to Sbiti. For a moment I was afraid lest he should be there waiting to confront me amongst the multi-coloured crowd that thronged the entrance, or upon the bare boards of the stairs, perhaps in the one iron lift that raised me unsteadily to the balcony where Zoboti's office could be found. But if he was there, he made no attempt to contact me, preferring perhaps to follow at a distance, or pursue other channels in his enquiries.

At any rate, I came upon the inevitable queue before Bureau 617, awaiting the chance of words with Sbiti's superior: seeking the nod from the man at the summit of the administrative pyramid. The door to the office was unprepossessing however; at some earlier stage it had been painted grey, but now the sun peeled the paintwork back in great scabs, and the office seemed suspended with a certain decrepit insecurity on the edge of the ministry, on the very edge of the very last balcony, the bureau number barely visible, the doorknob rusted and eaten away. It seemed altogether highly implausible; the crowd up there were silent and morose, a kind of hopeless awe seemed to have come upon them.

I tapped the last man in the queue lightly on the shoulder and asked him whether it was the queue to see Monsieur Zoboti, but his blood-veined eyes looked at me in a vague, barely seeing way, and his lips wrapped themselves loosely around a collection of almost inaudible syllables in reply. His face had been bleached by the sun to an unhealthy jaundiced shade of yellow, as if he had spent weeks out there exposed to the elements on the balcony, and white hairs of stubble pushed up through the flesh of his chin. I could see that he had no teeth, yet the cut of his djellaba showed him to be a man of some substance, but now apparently strangely fallen away. When finally he managed to gather the strength to speak, to dislodge his tongue from where it had rotted to the roof of his mouth, the words (those which I could catch) were in a dialect that I could not understand, and the move-

ments of his head seemed to indicate a negative and affirm-
ative answer to my question simultaneously. I asked him
again, but the man seemed capable only of glottal burblings,
as if blood were welling up at the back of his throat every
time that he tried to speak.

Growing impatient I moved past him and tackled the man
in front, a handsome, bronzed man in a well-cut suit, like
some Indian matinee idol, with great locks of curly hair, and
thick sexual lips that smiled stupidly. He carried one of those
fibreglass executive briefcases for which the keys can never
be found.

'Please, is this the queue to see Monsieur Zoboti?' I asked.

He grinned at me, a slow grin that spread faster along one
side of the face than the other, as if some rictus had momentarily gripped one of his cheeks. This quite destroyed my first
impression of him, and made him appear vaguely and irre-
parably flawed.

'Who knows Monsieur? One needs a guide in a place like
this, does one not?' he replied, and I was struck by the almost
total insincerity of what he had said, as if the smile were a
silent laugh both at himself and me, by some other more
honest person contained within his flashy exterior.

'Yes, it's true it's confusing, but perhaps you can tell me
where I might find Monsieur Zoboti?'

'Well, we all hope he is here, behind this door, or at least
I do. I do not talk to the others. You can't trust them, you
never know who they are, and unpleasant surprises are almost
inevitable at this level.'

When he said 'hope' it seemed to have a quite different
meaning to that normally associated with the word. Then he
launched into a long, almost prepared speech, all about his
problems (I had given him no encouragement), and concluded
with a crude demand for money. I excused myself and went
to the next person in the queue. I had no luck there either.
And so it went on:

'Who are you waiting for?'

'Is this Monsieur Zoboti's office?'

'Monsieur who?'

'Why are you queuing here?'

'That is surely none of your affair, Monsieur!'

The people shrugged, or waved their hands to show that they did not wish their silent concentration to be interrupted, or to show they did not know, until after other names had been mentioned, other conversations started and finished, I came to the very head of the queue, to the last man by the door. He opened his jacket to reveal a line of wristwatches, neatly pinned inside. I thought for one absurd moment they were trophies, symbolic medals of some obscurely surreal campaign, then lost my temper, pulled open the door to Zoboti's office and stepped inside.

There was a strong smell of paint and cheap cigarettes. Two men were whitewashing a small windowless room which was totally empty, except the floor, which was covered in old newspapers, crumpled in balls. The men stopped working and turned to look at me.

'*Il n'y a personne,*' they said. Through another door at the back I could see more bare floor and hear music, from a casette player or radio. A draught blew through this door, as if the windows in the room beyond had been opened to take away the smell of paint. I gestured vaguely towards the queue outside.

'There's a queue,' I said to the painters in the empty room.

'There's always a queue. This is a ministry after all. What can you expect?'

'But who are they waiting for?'

'Who knows? Maybe it is whoever was in here before. People come and go.'

'But shouldn't someone tell them?'

'Oh no, that's not our job. We're painters, only painters.'

'But some of them have been there for quite a long time.'

'So, if they want to queue, they can queue, can't they?'

I wrenched the door to the outside open again, and came face to face with the queue of people bunched around the door, their heads weaving from side to side as they tried to glimpse what was behind the door.

'There's nobody there. Monsieur Zoboti is not there,' I said. They looked at me blankly and tried to peer around the half closed door, to see what was in the room behind. I flung the door wide open and showed them the painters.

'You see, he's NOT THERE!'

Then one of those short fat ladies who always get to the front of crowds trilled at me angrily.

'Of course he is. It's just a trick to try our patience. If we wait long enough he will either come out or go in, and it is just a matter of time.'

The rest of the crowd murmured their approval of this theory.

'You're right, it's just a trick.'

'They're cunning people, right enough.'

I took the old lady by the wrist, such was my annoyance. How could they wait like that, in that endless hopeless way? I pulled her into the room where the painters were, but her curiosity was now replaced by fear.

'No! No, monsieur, if I do not wait, he will not come.'

I would not accept this extraordinarily subservient pessimism, maybe feared its development in myself. I pulled her further towards the inner office, behind the first office which I had entered, but inside there was another empty room and more newspaper on the floor, also crumpled.

'Do you see. He is not here and never will be,' I said to the woman. The painters laughed in the outer room and the old lady seemed bewildered and confused. Maybe that was what the waiting was for, maybe it was because waiting was less disappointing than arriving at the object of one's wait.

It was then, just as I was turning to leave, that I noticed the third door, in the corner, behind some of the decorators' ladders, and draped in red paint-splotched cloth. I felt suddenly stupid; maybe Zoboti was in there after all. I tried to lead the old lady from the room, but she stood there, still looking at the vacant office where Zoboti should have been. In a moment she would spot the third door, the hidden door, and demand to go behind it, become an encumbrance to my business in the way that Repair Man had become.

'Come on old lady. I am sorry I was so rough, but you see there is really no one there at all,' I said, guiding her steps into the outer room, where she stopped again to look at the painters.

'Please,' she asked. 'Is there a Monsieur Zoboti here?'

The painters sighed, as if they had heard the question many times before.

'No, there is no Zoboti,' they said, and she walked — almost teetered — from the room: back to rejoin the waiting crowd. I closed the door on her and heard her talking outside 'There is no Zoboti, the foreigner is right,' and the murmurs of disbelief:

'Well, where is the foreigner then, if there is no Zoboti? What is he doing in there? Writing letters to his uncle? Maybe he has deceived us. Maybe you are deceiving us.'

I heard no more because I had crossed the bare floor of the inner room, opened the third and final door, and found the elusive Zoboti at last.

Somehow, I had come upon him from an unexpected angle, and he had his back to me. Evidently there was some other more palatial entrance elsewhere. He was reading from *The Financial Times*, and his desk was littered with papers: great reams of printouts, armies of figures, containing the occasional handwritten correction. He spun on his swivel chair as I entered; a big man, with a jaw like a filing cabinet drawer, angry almost before he was surprised. Behind me, I could hear the painters trying to clear the crowd out of the outer office, where they had by now broken through to look for me.

'What foreigner? We have seen no one,' they said. The door I had entered by swung open with the wind from the windows, and Zoboti's papers began to drift, to blow on his great oaken tabletop. He strode straight past me, pulling a huge brass key from his djellaba, which he then inserted in the lock of the door, twisting it firmly the moment the door was closed. His movements had a massive air of control about them, as if his whole body operated to the dictates of some hidden mechanism, cast in bronze, and smoothly oiled.

'Narrator, I presume,' he said, and glided back to his chair, his feet noiseless on a great Berber rug, spotlessly white and yards across. I thought of dead sheep, a whole mountain flock, plucked from the green hillside above Zef. He boomed into the intercom system on his desk:

'I have a Monsieur Narrator here. I shall be five minutes only.' A frightened female voice squawked back at him with sudden truncated justifications.

'Keep the rear entrance locked in future would you,' he said, and switched her off and turned to me, where I still stood at the rear of his office, awkwardly trying to avoid stepping on the white carpet. I had the sudden notion that I was in the presence of power, and not merely the appearance of it which had somehow surrounded me since my arrival. It was as if all the energy, all the influence and all the self-confidence that others were lacking had somehow been sucked out of the country, off the streets, and up into this office with Zoboti and his complex researches. The entire office hummed with power, and every item in it represented knowledge or money or status, and this in itself seemed to seep into the very form of the man who now sat looking at me. He would never have chewing gum on the soles of his shoes nor let his digital watch go off in important meetings, and yet somehow the face was morose, heavily lined, without the patina of success. His sadness seemed to have made him bitter, and that had twisted the corners of his mouth downwards and made his eyes bulge.

'You are fortunate to have found the door, and it is only through politeness that I speak to you at all,' he said, as if to establish my inferiority right from the start. 'The doors help to keep people away and I have a secret entrance. It is all entirely necessary so that only the people who are desperate to get in will ever see me, or the people I myself wish to see.' He smiled gloomily, gaining some kind of depressive amusement from this knowledge, before continuing.

'I have had your files,' he said, sitting immobile, one hand on each knee, looking at me.

'I cannot understand why I have these problems, why they are not dealt with elsewhere. My staff are like virgins afraid to take the plunge, afraid to decide anything at all.' He seemed on the point of commenting further on this, but stopped himself, as if aware that his observations on human failings had become repetitive. He laid one hand out along the top of his desk, and his fingers played with a copy of *Le Figaro*, flicking the pages rhythmically. He seemed to be dealing with me obliquely, rambling, perhaps giving himself time to think.

'Monsieur Zoboti,' I began, but he cut me off brutally:

'Tell me, what hold did you have over Sbiti to get him to give you an appointment, to come up here snivelling to me? What had he done wrong that you had observed and threatened him with?'

'I do not know,' I said. I felt suddenly dirty, deflated in his presence.

'Was he talking about me? About the party? About the King? Maybe one of his friends was shouting out about these things. It fascinates me to hear details like this. I love to hear of hypocrisies , of people I know who say one thing to me, and then, when they are drunk, shout out something quite different.' He threw out suggestions to me, watching me, smiling. I tried to interrupt him, but he carried on:

'It doesn't matter, I mean after all, you cannot make me think this Sbiti is important.' I had a sudden picture in my mind of red pens, all over the building, red pens in painted nails, slashing through Sbiti's name, removing it from memoranda and affidavits, of the decorators moving into his old bureau and the windows open to let out the smell of the new paintwork.

'It is fascinating to me the way these matters are all related,' he said. 'Everything is connected in some way, and if you can make connections, of course I can make them too. I imagine this deal of yours, this pump–house, I imagine it is important to you, maybe as important to you as government is to me. Well, now that you are in the land of connections you must see that there is one linking your pump–house, Sbiti, and the necessity of maintaining correct attitudes amongst our people. I hope I am making myself clear. I am sorry my English is not as good as it was when I studied in Reading.'

The thought of Zoboti in Reading was alarming and astounding and ridiculous at one and the same time. Living in Reading he would not have been impressed. There would be no trading on cultural superiority now, because he would know how I thought, from days spent at Safeways Supermarket and the all-night disco at Annabel's. Worse, he would think he knew how I thought. Maybe he had been out with a girl from the council estate for a year or two. The whole revelation was a catastrophe. I said that I had understood what he was saying.

'Good,' he said, but I could see he was still waiting for me to speak. I opened my mouth, but the words would not come out. I could not even tell him about the pathetic Sbiti and his poor drunken friend, the unfortunate Monsieur Election. It was all just despair anyway, and I could not have people punished for that. Then he smiled at me, he even began to laugh, a sort of contemptuous, nasty laugh.

'My friend, why protect him? He is an obstacle to everything. He is an obstacle to efficiency, to progress. I have a Master's Degree in the economics of development; Sbiti to be frank, has nothing other than a father in the Ministry of Water and a lot of greedy relatives. Anyway, I see you will say nothing. It does not matter. Even by your silence he is condemned. Maybe I can see your principles, but I do not understand them. I cannot understand loyalty to a slug on the part of an educated man. I suppose it is amusing, in fact, yes, it definitely has that quality. I tell you what I will do Monsieur Narrator. I will let you have your pump-house, yes, I will let you have it, because the irony of our encounter has been entertaining for me, highly entertaining.' I felt like protesting, like challenging him, like saying that I was not being loyal to Sbiti, rather that I was not prepared to be loyal to Zoboti. I do not know at what point I had decided this in our conversation, or at what level within myself, but I was certain that no matter how much he intrigued me, I would not take Zoboti's side against Sbiti. Then, as he unlocked the door to bring the interview to an end, he said:

'The only problem about coming in this way is that you have also to go out through it. We cannot have people coming out through entrances which they have not entered by.' He shook my hand and I saw, barely visible on his lapel, the upside down parrot that I had seen in the newspaper photograph in Goughly, when the whole affair had started.

'Ah, the parrot,' he said. 'The parrot is a mystery and mystery is power in the land of the curious.' He smiled and closed the door, sealing himself in his office with his paper-work. When he had done this, and when I found myself once again in the empty outside room, I felt strangely deserted, as if even in our brief unpleasant encounter, we had established some kind of close relationship. But then that is how people can come to power.

I walked back through the empty room. One of the painters was still painting, ignoring me, and I turned to him on impulse:

'Why did you tell me there was no one here,' I asked.

He turned on his ladder.

'Because there is no one here. Monsieur Zoboti has said so,' he said, and continued painting rhythmically, the brush slip-slapping across the bare walls. 'After all, Monsieur, you yourself told them the same thing,' he added.

When I opened the outer door, the crowd ignored me quite resentfully. I heard them muttering angrily:

'He knows how to see Zoboti; he is a foreigner. Of course they have advantages,' while other voices murmured in dissent. 'Maybe he is just appearing to have seen him, just pretending. Maybe he knows the painters . . .' I walked past quickly, until the old-man — the one I had first spoken to — pulled at my sleeve, until he tried to follow, his voice cracked and hard to follow in an Arabic he had now discovered.

'Please, please Monsieur, can I see him? Can you take me to him, can you show me the secret room?'

I bent down and whispered in his ear. 'The room is easy. It is at the back of the second room and all you have to do is knock on the door behind the stepladder.' He stopped, looked at the queue and then at me. Then he looked at the queue and I could see that he did not believe me.

After my encounter with Zoboti I experienced no sense of exhilaration or relief, no great sigh escaped my lips as I slipped out under the decorated arches of the ministry; rather, there was a sudden flatness within, like a canal on a grey windless day in some Northern city on a winter Sunday. I walked away down the boulevard. Two large mercedes taxis had collided on a roundabout and the drivers were arguing, pushing each other, about. Slight scurries of fine dust lifted from the pavement and the boulevard seemed to drift along under my feet, with no apparent effort, as if I were being carried by a slow moving invisible train.

A beggar sailed across my path, tugged at my sleeve, lacking an eye. I gave him a five dirham note and passed on. The deal was probably settled now, but for the authorisation itself; no doubt it would come in the post today, tomorrow, or in a few weeks. Thoughts came upon me: urges, inspirations, with no order in them, contradictorily. I felt an urge to pack, to go home to Goughly and then, minutes later, an urge to stay in Tabar for a day or two, and maybe take a taxi down to the coast to one of the fishing villages, to swim and enjoy the fine white beaches. Then I thought about drinking, maybe contacting Munton; considered it, then abandoned it and settled for an indecisive coffee on the terrace of the first café I came to.

No sooner had I sat down and ordered than the girl came upon me. I heard a voice behind me.

'*Salut Narrator, comment vas-tu?*' She was dressed in white (brown skin, a birthmark), and I knew things would begin again. She smelt vaguely of sunlight, or how one imagined sunlight would smell, somehow cleaner that it was possible to be. She sat beside me and slightly behind me, so that I had to twist my head to look at her, though I could sense her there like an impending electric storm. If she had been invisible I would have known immediately that she was there.

'What have you been up to? I went to your hotel to find you,' she said. 'I guessed you might be doing business.'

I found that Murphy's text had suddenly come to dominate my thinking again, found that I could barely speak to her.

'Well, what's happened to you? Why so gloomy?'

I turned to her. Her shirt was half unbuttoned, the swelling of her breasts, a gold chain between.

'Have you seen Murphy?' I asked.

'That *salop!* What a waste of time he is. I've told you before what I think of him. What should I have to do with him? After all, he's a drunken brute. Is that what is worrying you?' She laughed brightly and she giggled, with her hand in front of her face. Her eyes seemed to giggle too, a kind of nervous, fearful merriment.

'How does he know about us?' It was difficult for me to even phrase the question.

'What has he been saying? Have you seen him?' she asked. 'Obviously he has been saying something, otherwise you would not be so cross.' Then she became furious:

'What has he been saying about me. Tell me. He has been saying something, Narrator. That bastard, he will destroy us. Tell me what he has been saying, please!'

Then reluctantly, I told her about the strange text; merely the barest details, and she became silent and thoughtful, a sort of cunning look on her face, considering motives, or elements of which I was only vaguely aware.

'You know what he's doing Narrator. You know he is trying this to split us apart. He is jealous in some way. That is what is at the root of it, the *salop* wants me back, he wants to sleep with me.' She smiled at the thought, then laughed gaily again.

'How did he know? Have you seen him? What have you told him? Oh no, you people you are filth, the lowest kind of filth I know.'

'I haven't seen him, or talked to him, or written, or told him anything,' I said, then added 'Maybe you have.'

'How can I! I have not seen him. What do you take me for? I think it is you. I am not surprised; this is the way with friends, this is the way they repay you; you show them love, and they blab about it everywhere, spew it all out to their friends.'

'But it doesn't make any sense Maria,' I said. I was vaguely excited by all this. Despite myself, I was overcome by a curious kind of fetishism, built around her scent and the very foreignness of the conversation. I did not really care.

'The world is full of toads. It is not really surprising that they croak now and again,' she said, then began to attack me again.

'You did not seriously think that I would tell Murphy? That is too much. You really thought that I would tell him everything that we did together? What do you take me for? Do you take me for a whore? That is the most dreadful thing, far worse than anything Murphy could do. Who knows? Maybe it is just an accident. Why blame me for accidents? Why blame me for the depravities of one of your friends? *On a rien fait ensemble, absolument rien!*'

She began a tirade, in the way that people here do, and I began to smile at her, and then quite suddenly she laughed, catching my smile, abandoning her whole argument in mid sentence.

'It's all too stupid,' she said. Then we paid up and walked out into the street, with my arm around her waist. She was still a little tense, as if the feelings within her had all come too quickly, and had been locked together before they could be given full expression. We walked on slowly, towards the hotel, and as we walked, we argued.

'Where did you go last night when you left me?' I asked, seeking leverage, some position from which I could hold her, prise open her defences.

'Why do you want to know?'

'I just wondered.'

'I went to my sister's.'

'In Bar es Medina?' I mentioned the poor immigrant district I had followed her to.

'How did you know that?'

'I followed you.'

'Humph. I see. Again you have not the slightest confidence in me.' She had become flat and toneless.

'It is not that I do not have confidence, it's just that I have curiosity, that's all. You can't expect to create mysteries and then not have people try to unravel them.'

'But there are no mysteries. I have told you everything. I live with my sister, with my sister and her husband. He has a good job. I have told you about that and I have told you about the children and everything. I have told you about the Sanyo video recorder, the berber rugs. If you choose not to believe me then that is your concern. It is just that if you do so you will lose me, utterly. The choice is yours.'

We walked on more slowly, our bodies out of step. She took shorter steps than before, and her shoulders jarred against me, slowing me down. She had set me an ultimatum now, and I was entrapped in a verbal game, a mock fencing match, which I could accept or reject as I fancied. Whatever happened my mind would need to be made up by the time her pace had slowed to a standstill. She seemed determined.

'But why can't you just tell me what you were doing out there?'

'Narrator, you have a choice in this you know, so think carefully before you answer. Either you believe me or I say goodbye to you here on the spot, and it will be goodbye. You will never see me again and it will be the end of everything.' She talked in clichés; they even seemed to give her a curious satisfaction, as if she were only happy with established phrases and her entire conversation were designed to give her the opportunity to slip them into the argument. Then we came to a standstill and I was vaguely aware of the noise of traffic, the passage of people around, the crowds pushing past. She hung her head, and her hair fell down over her eyes. One hand was now hooked dejectedly in my shirtfront.

'But it would be simpler if you told me,' I said. I did not know why I wanted her to admit to poverty, to squalor, to desperation, perhaps at heart I still did not trust her, maybe did not even like her.

'No. Do you believe me or not? That is all I am asking you. Do you think I am a liar?' She began to turn away from me, slowly, in a careful determined sort of way.

'Of course I believe you.'

As I said this, she hugged me with astonishing force there in the middle of the street, so strongly that I nearly fell over, quite unexpectedly.

'I'm glad. I'm so glad Narrator. I thought you too suffered from the great distrust.'

The scales had been neatly tipped by the very tightness of her jeans, the tip-tap of her heels, her keenness for my support for her dreams, her determination to have some false expression of trust from me.

And so we walked on down a long street of open-fronted carpet shops with great rugs in ochre, gold and purple; cascading down from wooden balconies, displayed there in the sunlight for their gaudy opulence to fade, with the shop owners watching for rain from the cool interiors where they sipped their tea.

'Do you have carpets like that in your country?' She asked.

'Not really,' I said, and then began to talk about England as I remembered it; the strange ugly people, the vacuous conversations, while she listened with her head slightly on one side. I explained afternoon tea, and she giggled. She said she thought it sounded bourgeois. She had seen people like us in films and she had heard our polite conversations.

'It is different,' I said.

She said we seemed no happier than anyone else.

'You are not happy people, with your fast new cars and your briefcases.'

'It's the weather. It rains all the time.'

'I shouldn't like that. It makes you all miserable and greedy and unable to give.'

'I am not greedy nor particularly unhappy,' I said.

'Well, why do you spend your time with me then? There are thousands of other women who you could go with, and yet you choose to stroll with me and let me insult you.'

I became tired of this continual delving, the searching for weaknesses, the criticism.

'I haven't a clue why I walk with you,' I said.

'Humph!' She said.

We came upon the hotel, this time from a different angle, through some side streets with which she was already apparently well acquainted. We slid up to the door via an alley full of cats, a silence on both of us, and climbed the stairs with a dream-like lassitude. The desk-boy smiled cheerfully.

'How are we today?' He asked. 'It's a great day for a swim!' He tendered us the key for the room up near the roof without being asked. As I climbed, the lassitude became greater, and my legs began to feel as if the muscles had somehow been chopped half through at the point where they connected with the bones. Maria hung on my arm, and the added weight slowed us still further. On the final landing we stopped and she slowly, gently began to kiss my neck. The landing was hot. We were both sweating. The hotel was quite silent, except for the gentle noise of her lips and the occasional creaking of the joists in the roof under the sun. We kissed there for some time, suspended in the heart of the city, my hands up under the back of her shirt, where the perspiration had collected, making her back smooth and almost oily. We began to climb again, the stairs dark and ill-lit. When we reached the corridor I began to unbutton her shirt, imagining her there, naked, drifting down this secret passageway, hidden from the city. Her hands slipped into my trousers and the door to the room swung open. It was still musty inside, the curtains were drawn, and the sun shone through the thin material making strange patterns on the walls and the bedspread. We lay on the bed, exploring each other.

'What do you like, Narrator?' she asked.

I felt lazy, somehow unconvinced by everything, as if part of the text written by someone else, estranged from myself and reality at one and the same time. An awful creeping loneliness came upon me as she explored my body, now more skilfully. I felt her hands as an intrusion, something reaching from reality into the dream of the novel in which I had become entrapped. I pulled away and stood up, my organ faintly ridiculous, my trousers at halfmast, while she moved on the bed.

'*Viens me baiser*,' she said. When I looked at her she was lying spread across the bed, with her body, streaked in sweat, almost posing. Her eyes were half closed and she breathed lightly, a strange, mysterious, corrupt temple stirred by the faintest of breezes. One hand lay over her face, hiding her teeth.

'*Qu'est-ce- que tu fais? Viens me baiser.*' Her voice was lazy, slightly bored. I took off the rest of my clothes, and felt my own nakedness and her body waiting there, splashed by the light from the window. I moved towards her, suddenly attracted, and then the sudden shock of entry, a total, complete entry . . . She shouted, she pulled my hair, the obscenities, the wild rage came again, the fury that somehow seemed to block all satisfaction, the terrible search in both of us, and then the wrenching climax that left a feeling of something stolen, something half given and half taken, something tantalising that made us grip each other tightly until our joints ached long after it was over.

'Will you take me to England?' she asked in the end. Her voice was muffled in my chest.

'Is that what you want?'

'I don't know.' Her hands gripped my shoulders, clenching and unclenching.

'You said you wouldn't like the rain.'

'You did not attempt to persuade me otherwise.'

'I do not know you. Still I don't know you.'

'It is not important. A lot of people do not know each other, and yet they live together quite happily. Anyway, what is it that you want to know about me?'

I could not think what it was; it was something so nonspecific, like a fog on a country road which obsures everything, so the eye cannot even begin to seek the country field, the pillar boxes, the bus stops, and one's eyes report nothing but illusions in the mist, can seek nothing other than objects lodged in the memory.

'You can ask me anything,' she said.

'That's the problem.'

'Ha!'

'What makes you so ... so angry?'

'Is that all. I can answer that quite simply. I have always been like that. In fact my mother's maid said that I was the worst child she had ever had to deal with. I was dreadful and thoroughly vicious. One day (she laughed as she remembered), I sent a beggar under a bus. Can you believe that? I was standing on the balcony and a blind beggar was in the street below, shouting up for money. I pretended to throw him some down and shouted out to him that I had thrown it. He scrabbled around in the dirt by the roadside, and I shouted out instructions. "Left a bit, right a bit, no ... go forward", and I led him out into the road and the mail bus knocked him down. There was no money, don't you see, no money at all.' She stopped, as if listening in her imagination for the sound of bones crunching.

'So you think that I am bad?'

'I don't think so,' I said. I had found her story unconvincing, as if she were writing her own part, her own character as she went along, according to whim.

'What does your sister's husband do?' I watched her.

'This and that. Business.'

'What kind of business?'

'Oh, I don't know. This and that like most people, I suppose. He is often tired, and earns a lot of money.' To all my questions there was an answer with form but without any kind of substance. Her eyes caught mine from time to time, very dark, almost black, unnaturally bright as if she had been crying, or drinking.

I rolled off the bed, and was about to wash myself in the sink, when I recalled Murphy's text. Maybe if I could create some small detail that would not be ignored, that would catch them, if indeed they were there to catch. I pulled on my clothes, and tried to think of something distinctive that could be done, something that would have to appear in any future text. My mind however was blank, and this depressed me as

I washed under my armpits, whistling tunelessly as I did so. I abhorred the idea of another blank and flabby farewell. Then I had an idea. I turned to her, knelt down and kissed her sex.

'*Qu'est ce que tu fais?*' she said, surprised. '*Tu es un vrai salop, tu sais!*'

'You will write to me so that we can meet again?' I asked.

'Oh yes. I'll write. You will hear soon — tomorrow evening.'

I said goodbye to her and closed the door quietly and listened for a moment. I could hear her running water in the sink and singing quietly, a wailing, eery, Arabic sound.

Much later, back at my hotel I found that the lingering urge to depart was still there: the urge to pack, to fold my things, empty the cupboards. This was a process that always gave me satisfaction; it was a kind of continuous process of disappearing, a way of tempting others to call out to me, to beg me to stay or to return, and yet it never really happened. I still felt somehow burdened by a sense of absurdity. Absurdity I know should be a lightening sensation, but events recently had gone beyond this. They had long ago reached that point where one reacted with detachment, for I had been through this period. I felt I was now approaching the period of horror. I began to wonder if there were any further position one could reach.

I picked at the paper in a desultory way, Zoboti was in there again, addressing another conference. It was in fact the same conference photo that I had seen in Goughly, only the caption was different. He seemed to be looking out at me, inviting me to approve, as if I were there before him in the very front row of his audience.

I called in on Munton at his office the next day to give him the news about the pump–house deal. It was part of a familiar process of finishing up, as if in telling him that the deal was concluded it would be erased from my memory, and new business could then be taken on with a fresh and uncluttered mind.

He had an office above a large stationery shop in one of the principal boulevards, and the previous director of the Société Herzog had invested in a neon sign announcing 'Herzog-Importations', which flashed on and off in the window. Unfortunately bits of the sign no longer functioned, and it attracted flies — had done so for quite a time — and they lay there in the bottom of the perspex case like sheep droppings, simmering in the flickering neon light.

Munton however was cheerful, even a little incredulous, when I told him how I had squeezed Sbiti and finally cleared the import order with Zoboti. Already it seemed to have faded in my memory, though the queue was still there, quite vividly. He shook his head up and down approvingly.

'That's great! Quite excellent! A useful contact for us ...' and so on, he said. He did not mention the 12% commission that he personally stood to gain from the deal, nor necessarily the uninterrupted weekend in some off-season mountain hotel where he would no doubt go with some girl now that it was all over. He was still enough of an Englishman to want to have tangible achievements before he would allow himself tangible rewards.

I suggested that Sbiti's future was no longer secure as a result of the clearance we had obtained. He said he thought it was a bloody good thing, that he had never been particularly taken by the man.

'Law of the jungle. All in the same boat you know,' he said, looking at his watch to see if it was late enough for the first drink of the day, vaguely disappointed when he discovered that it was not.

'Fancy some lunch later?' He asked, but I turned him down. I had to pack, I was going soon anyway. I would see him in Goughly one day.

'Doubt it very much,' he said, saying goodbye to me on the steps.

'Thanks for everything. I'll drop the clearance over.'

'It's nothing. It keeps me out of mischief.' He smiled wanly, even paler in the full light of the sun. I crossed the street, looked back and waved to him, but he did not see me because he was again checking his watch.

Then the vague gloom that I had experienced the previous day descended on me. The man without appointments always seems to notice the least cheerful and desirable things in himself, and these came upon me suddenly, as if waiting for just such a moment when the necessities were no longer there to keep them away. I hurried towards the Metropole, determined now to pack, to begin to move, to at least have a panorama travelling past, some spurious progress, some distraction, but as I climbed the stairs I realised there were some difficulties involving the documents, the paperwork that Munton would need so that ships could actually be loaded and generators swung onto quaysides so that something could actually be built. I would have to wait for the papers to come through.

At the landing outside my room I stopped, in a generalised quandary, which I rapidly began to interpret as a weakness of character. It was then that I resolved to get myself anonymously and spectacularly drunk, something which I seldom did. This time the situation seemed right in almost every way, and I entered my room to collect some extra money. It always required extra money to buy drinks, food, tickets, taxis, medical treatment and things one left behind. The urge to drink could not be put off by considering the exact items one needed to take along; they would just have to be bought as the need arose. However, as I opened the drawer of my bedside table where I kept my money, I noticed on top, under the lampstandard, a brown envelope of a familiar pattern, a pattern I had seen before; one of those envelopes without glue, that one seals with a wire tie, a kind of envelope one uses for the despatch of manuscripts, in fact the kind of envelope Murphy had used before. Inside there were several typed sheets, pinned neatly together as on the last occasion, and I read standing up.

'The fat salesman sat at the table spending his money on the girl. She sat behind him so she would not have to look at him, look at his face, see his watery eyes. He kept twisting in his seat so that he could see her breasts, which she knew excited him. She could almost smell his physical excitement, expected at any moment for him to begin dribbling, or quivering into his coffee. She detested and despised him, as she unbuttoned her shirt still further so that he could torment himself further with the morality of making love with someone who had betrayed him. He licked his lips, flecked with coffee. She smiled at him, always behind him so that she did not have to look at him. The game was really to destroy him now, and she knew the tight-clenched debasing anger in him by the way he made love, she knew now that he would never really give her anything. So she was setting out to destroy him, by the very act of love itself — which he paid for as a method of restoring his self-esteem — she would destroy him, catch him utterly and pull out the wobbly gut-like foundations of his morality, of his soul. She longed to make him break up. She taunted him there in the café, insulted him, played with him, leaning forward, letting her breasts hang provocatively, touching him.

Then, when the anger came she would attack him on some pretext or other. He thought she was a whore! The humour of this situation was almost too much for her. Both of them had to pretend that this was not the case when both of them knew that that was what she was. It was truly remark-able. She made sure when she walked that he could see her bottom, and she had put on her slenderest high heels, so she could excite him with those minor, ridiculous fetishes that fat old men tend to have, so she could push him away with her anger and then haul him back with the click-clack of her heels, her swaying hips, her long thighs.

She could give him just enough of her personality to make it impossible for him to fuck her as he would an animal, just enough doubt to cripple any enjoyment he might have. Apparently he had been following her (jerking off in his trousers no doubt), to see where she lived. She would not admit she lived where he had followed her to and stuck to her original story absurdly. She forced him to say he believed her, and he hung there, flabby and whey faced, lacking even the elementary determination to stick by what his eyes had seen. She let her hand hang in his shirt front, let him feel her fingers, her breasts against him, mock appealing, and that was enough to swing him. He began to ramble on about England, about the luxuries of life there. Could he not see the temptation for her in this?'

I stuffed the papers into my jacket pocket, and set off down the stairs, two at a time, then three, and left the hotel so fast that I nearly ran under one of those great drays, ducked past the horses and across the road and away up a maze of labyrinthine alleys, at first with absolutely no clear idea of where I was going. If anyone had stood in my path, I would have killed them. I was full to overflowing with a desire for revenge, a sort of furious violence, a desire for revenge both on myself and on the girl and on Murphy and the country, if only I could find them.

I ran towards the quarter where she lived, or where I thought she lived, the text bundled together with my money. It was the very intimacy of the conversations that Maria and Murphy must have had in order to write it that was the most shocking. I took a taxi, babbling angrily at the driver, who manoeuvred around the city traffic with painful and infuriating slowness, stopping at every red light. Maybe the perceptions were Murphy's rather than the girl's, and the details had been fleshed out through his distorted vision of corruption, their two viewpoints wedded together? I could not think why they were doing this. Anything was possible with Murphy, but what was the girl's contribution? Had I known all along that she was a prostitute?

The taxi arrived at the alley in Bar es Medina, the alley which I had followed her to once before. Perhaps that was the cause of it? I jumped out without paying, returned and tipped lavishly. It was the early afternoon, and a hot grey mist hung over the streets, enveloping the decay, making the sweat run into my eyes. Some small boys again played in the street.

'Do you know a girl called Maria who lives here? She is a tall girl, with black hair and steel teeth.' They looked blankly, smiled blankly. An old woman nearby swabbed down her doorstep, and I called over to her, receiving the same kind of slow response.

'There are many girls like that here, Monsieur.'

She began scrubbing the steps energetically.

One man I asked smiled, showing blackened stumps where his teeth should have been.

'You wan' girl? I get you girl. I get you good girl,' while another further down the street turned and shouted angrily.

'Hey you! What for you cause us troubles, eh? What fo' you come here?' And a crowd began to assemble, from nowhere, out of the mist. I began to feel my foreignness keenly, the legacy of other visits by other men perhaps.

'You wan' jig-jig?' Shouted a group of youths, and the people laughed. One of those great father–figures, white-bearded and massive, perhaps the district head man, came towards me with a monkey wrench in his hand.

'Go back where you came from. Don't bother us. Go back!'

His big voice boomed around the street, echoing from the flaking whitewashed walls, and I backed off, the crowd now some twenty strong following me. I turned and began to walk away and they shouted out.

'What fo' you not like good clean girl?' And laughed again.

Someone threw a stone, and I turned and began to walk away. At the end of the street I caught a taxi, and as it pulled away I could see the crowd at the junction, some of them angry, shaking their fists.

When we had driven far enough, I had the driver drop me at the first bar I could safely drink in. It was on the corner of a large vegetable market, now closed for lunch break, and the smell of overripe vegetables mingled with the smell of beer. The bar was dark and moist inside, almost cool. The counter was unusually high and wide to prevent customers assaulting the staff, the walls bare and patched in places; it was a good place to start. Men from the market sat at iron tables painted in different colours, with the rust showing through the paint. Some played cards or draughts. In one corner, a customer snored loudly, the noise of his sleep rumbling overhead like distant thunder, while two others carried on a conversation over his recumbent form as if he were not there. The place had the necessary anonymity, the necessary sense of nowhere in particular. An old advertisement for orange juice was tacked to the wall with outsize nails, fading, showing a girl with blonde hair and large thighs, a full white skirt, laughing, large-eyed. '*Buvez Chouki!*' I ordered a large Pernod and chose a seat in the corner. The chair I had picked upon would not sit straight on the uneven concrete floor, and the table wobbled, with one leg curiously bent back on itself. Clients had scratched their names in the paintwork, the names of girls. Naima, Rachida, even Maria, maybe the same girl under different disguises, different identities. I demolished the Pernod and ordered a brandy from the special bottle over the photos of the bar-owner's family. I was attracting some attention now, not even invisible. I pulled out the text again, once I felt the alcohol beginning to work.

'Then came the awful climb in the hotel, the feeling of dread, his laboured breathing like a pig truffling for something in a muddy farmyard and the smell of his sweat, old sweat and unwashed shirt, the dreadful fawning of the man on the door. For a moment she doubted whether he would actually go through with it again. He stopped. She forced herself to arouse him, to touch his body, to engage the primitive gears, to set the engine going. Murphy would write it as it should be written, and that was the consolation, the reward, if only she could be there to see his face, his big flabby lips . . . the round 'O' of amazement and the directionless apoplectic anger. She would leave him alone until the vengeance faded, then start again and again, and continue until she had debased him to the furthest possible level, to the level of the utterest and most final text. He was that kind of man, the kind that would suffer the most from exactly that kind of exposure. The humour of it came upon her, and she became light-hearted and began to arouse him, amused that he thought he was gaining something from the transaction, when in fact it was the very reverse; something was being stolen from him, taken away.

"What do you like?" She felt excited now.

"Come and fuck me," she said and he waddled over. There was that odd enjoyment in it which began to worry her, which increased as she became aware of his difficulties; so she fought against the enjoyment and held back, felt him splurt up there and collapse against her. Then she began to dream of the first intention that had lain behind it all, the intention that always lay behind it.

"Will you take me to England?" she asked.

It was not important anyway. She invented another character for herself, told him some strange story that drifted into her head, about a beggar and how he had been killed by accident, by an accident of her making (make it threatening, just a little chilling). It was quite possible she could have done that, and quite by accident too. Still he sought what he had not found in fucking her, despite the story, despite everything, still he questioned her, trying to have part of her for himself that he could be certain of. She continued to elude him, to evade him. Then, when he left her he did something odd; he knelt and kissed her sex. It gave her an eery feeling, a slight doubt, a worry that perhaps in his mind somewhere there lurked a secret, romantic, creative corner. It did not matter as what she was doing would probably finish with that. Once he had left, she sang lightheaded. Maybe there was nothing you could do to stifle romance.'

How much of this was Murphy and how much Maria? This question bubbled up through the babble of other questions in my mind, the bar distant, once again as if through some kind of plate glass. Maybe she did not see that these texts could give me some kind of power, if I could only make my influence dominant over Murphy's in her mind. If she would love me a little I could hit back at him, at them. Maybe, if I could not do this, there was some disease that I could spread through her to him, to strike at their mental decay with something that matched it on the physical side? There would have to be something, and as I sat there enclosed in the warm, fruity interior of the bar, wrapped in drink, almost anything seemed attractive, even the most disgusting things. I folded the text and ordered a further drink.

Then I fumbled my money, and dropped it on the floor. The waiter picked it up, expressionless. A commotion started up by the door. A man was trying to get in, and there was some shouting in a voice that I recognised. I glimpsed a huge pink teddy bear with green eyes and thought for one terrifying moment that my sanity had gone. I mumbled something to the waiter. The man was now wedged in the swing doors, and began kicking at them. The other barman moved anxiously towards him and the man burst through, finally recognisable as an excessively drunken Sbiti, with a huge fairground toy under his arm. The other drinkers laughed. Sbiti saw the danger in the approaching barman, and miraculously pulled himself upright, organised the teddy bear, and spotted me with the characteristic perceptiveness of the drunk at sea.

'Ahaaaaa!' he said over loudly, pointing at me. No barman would interfere with a customer who was drunk but with a friend, as the friend could always be relied upon to do the right thing. The bar staff could relax, until the friend became drunk as well. Sbiti now took advantage of this, and teetered magisterially towards me and sat down. He placed the teddy bear on the seat opposite, from where it sat staring greenly at the orange juice advert until the end of our conversation. The waiter hovered.

'This man will buy me a drink,' said Sbiti.

'Beer,' I said.

'Ahaa,' said Sbiti again, and suddenly burst into song. The waiter moved forward menacingly and Sbiti stopped. The waiter retreated again, obediently,

'Y'see. Control of waiters by song,' said Sbiti. His shirt front had been unbuttoned and rebuttoned in the wrong order, and he wore no tie, no jacket. Somewhere in his passage he had fallen over.

'I do not bear a grudge,' he said, after a period of silence during which his face had worked itself through the gamut of available expressions.

'I grudge no one. No one at all.' I could not work out exactly what had happened to him. Someone had untied one of the knots that had kept his pompous being together.

'No grudge at all. *Que sera sera.* You know this song?' He began to sing, but I motioned to him to keep quiet.

'This is the strength, the strength Narrator. The strength of our people, the great people of this country. We are not the ones for the bearing of grudges. You know what I mean?' I said I wasn't clear.

'No grudges borne. In the last campaign against the partisans, what did we do when the world was against us?' I said I did not know.

'We did NOTHING! NOTHING AT ALL! A petty diplomatic protest, a note at some macaroon session in Paris. That is the strength of our country.' He seemed utterly convinced by this theory, in the way that drunks have.

'You are talking about the war in the desert?'

'Yesh. Absolutely. Shhhhhhh!' He gestured for calm and began on a whispered monologue that was almost incomprehensible.

'Many problems ... of course they had the Kalashnikovs and by God they could fight. And, this is the crux ... what did we do? We did nothing! We sat there in the towns, down bolt holes in Sidi Boulmein and Tinjlit, watching them through binoculars. Of course, far be it from me ... of course I believe that to have been right, with hindsight. Be quiet; that is precisely the thing to aim for. Be quiet and there will be no trouble. Let them blow your bollocks off. Yes, even that

Narrator. Stay with the family. The family is everything. Stay with the family, the mother. My mother is a marvellous woman. I should have stayed with her . . . solid, like this.' He clenched his fist impressively and I nodded.

'What do I care. The ministry is nothing to me! NOTHING! We never needed one before, so why do we need one now? By God, when the French were here these chaps weren't worth a fart. Administration? Dogshit! No . . . I do not hold any grudges.'

'But what has happened Sbiti?'

'My job, my office, all gone. There this morning and the decorators were in. Lime green, can you imagine that, all my secretaries gone. By God they were goers . . . inherited them from Mechbal before me, the under-secretary. Cunts like melons. Imagine that.'

'So you've changed your office?'

'Changed it? Of course I've changed it. Changed it for the street, for the alley and the backstreets and the brothel. Didn't I say change was the object of the exercise. We come, we go, but change endures . . . I am a philosopher am I not?'

'But why so drunk? Your job has gone?'

'Drunk. I'm not drunk, how dare you. I'm jush a liddle tired, that's all. Just tired, can y'see that. God yes, d'you know that chap you asked about? What was his name? The cousin of that scoundrel you brought to see me. Silly thing to do really.' I nodded.

'Well, he's back again, a bit thinner, a bit more thoughtful, he's back on my swivel chair. Justice in a way. Never liked the chair, needed too much oiling.'

'And you?'

'Well, I am here, am I not? That is all you can say, really all that anyone can say. I went to see Zoboti, but he was out, away, in conference. They did not positively tell me to go, you understand; they just would not tell me where I had my office. Where can I work? I asked. "I do not know, Monsieur Sbiti. There are accommodation problems." I must have an office to do my work, I said. "If you do no work you need no office for the moment," they replied. I checked with salaries to find that my name had already been crossed off. In fact they wouldn't even speak to me when they found my name wasn't on the list.'

We ordered more drinks and he said how glad he was to have met me.

'It is like a test. A test for me. How much can Sbiti take? You see my meaning. After all it is quite absurd, absurd in every way, to sit here drinking with you. I will spend all my money. Yes I will spend it all very quickly, so that I will have none to spend in the places where I was known. Known, but not well-known. I was not a bar-vulture. Never. Never let it be said. Hey! Narrator! Let's get some girls: two, maybe three. I know a girl with a fabulous bum, just fabulous. We take her, you and I? After all, it is the last time I will be seen talking like this. Soon dishonesty will be compulsory just to make ends meet, and I'll have to fawn and scrape like your friend, the scoundrel. What did he do? Some kind of *petit commerçant* perhaps? It doesn't matter anyway; we are all men after all. Come on, lets go to the whorehouse and find a pretty girl with nipples like black cherries, dark and suckable. You have to go to the end Narrator, to the very end. People who stop do not understand. Look at life from every angle: from the top, the middle and the bottom.' He looked around the bar and turned to the teddy bear.

'It is the bottom my friend, my only true friend. Say hello to Monsieur Narrator.' He waved the teddy bear's arm at me, and smiled the same smile as Monsieur Election had done. Then he dropped suddenly between his chair and the teddy bear, felled by drink. He tried to get up, groaned, and lay down full length on the floor amongst the cigarette ends. The teddy bear seemed to peer down at him now, the green plastic eyes impassive.

By now the afternoon was closing in, and the bar had emptied. The noise of the market could be heard outside, the gathering momentum of business in fruit and vegetables. I bent over Sbiti, but he was breathing regularly. I tried to wake him, but he murmured angrily that I should go away, that I should leave. I called over the barman to help me, and he stood there looking down, unimpressed and unmoved, Sbiti's recumbent form a reproach to me, a friend who had not done his duty, someone who had let his drinking partner fall to the floor. I bent down and tried to pick him up, but all his muscles were limp and he sagged like a sack of bananas.

'You had better leave him. He has had too much,' said the barman. I lifted him up however, with one final effort, just far enough to be able to prop him on a seat. The barman bent down and picked up Sbiti's cigarettes where they had fallen, took two out and lit them, handing one to me. Sbiti was slumped on the table, snoring, mumbling in his sleep, the words 'go ... go away ... leave ...' coming out irregularly from some point inside him, independent of his slumbers. This was frustrating.

I ordered another drink and sat at the table, looking at him, looking at his slightly repellent face, fallen away in sleep. I felt stupid now, sitting, drinking with my partner unconscious, dimly aware that my behaviour was not what was expected of a European. I got up and left the bar, leaving half my drink just out of Sbiti's reach, so that he would not knock it over when he awoke.

I cannot remember all the bars, except that for most of the time I was moving, climbing up towards the walled city which overlooked the estuary. Even in confusion I set myself some ultimate objective; the blue mosque appeared and re-appeared on street corners, between buildings, perched on the rock overlooking the city, its tower fading against the darkening sky, until all that could be seen of it was the blinking of the light that had been fixed to it to warn off low flying aircraft.

There were many bars, with torn seats, ragged upholstery, ragged conversation, argument that trailed meaninglessly, meandered, was cut short or larded with importunings, entreaties, theories. In every bar there were people with knowledge to unburden, like caverns full of the waste of the country's soul, the strange deceits, the stratagems and discoveries.

'Do you know the wife of the President is a Russian! I swear it is true. Monsieur. Look ...' (a newspaper unfurled, yellow at the edges, maybe a page from a popular magazine) and then the inevitable 'Of course the world is damned, utterly damned. It is because we turn our backs on the Lord. You do. I know you do. Look at this glass in my hands, already empty ...' and always there was a pulling away, the hands clutching.

'But wait, Monsieur, surely there is time for another drink,' and the restless desire to halt the talk, the flood of words, by moving again; the feeling that maybe all the conversations plunged away into a reason that was utterly absurd, a reason which could drive one mad oneself. At one point I became suddenly faint, and the street sloped away at an odd angle, seeming briefly to be trying to knock me over by its sudden movements beneath my feet.

I came to a small fountain, playing in a square, and dipped my head under the rushing water again and again until it cleared. Every girl I passed I looked at closely. Sometimes the look was misunderstood, and girls offered themselves, or the reverse, and their brothers materialised threateningly at my elbow. At one point I felt I was being followed, but could see no one. I bought a bracelet of silver chain ('but Monsieur, it is an incomparable bargain') then lost it, or had it stolen, and wasted an hour or so aimlessly looking for it in the cracks of the cobbles, cursing myself as I did so.

Then finally, as night fell, I came up against the mosque, its walls intricately, tiled, smooth blue tiles, cool in the evening breeze as I ran my hand across them. From the ledge over-hanging the cliff which fell away into the estuary, I looked out at the sea. Other lone figures stood there too, looking out to where the river met the ocean, where the breakers piled up and swept in, the sea rolling over the river. Then the sky turned pink, pinkish blue and darkened quite suddenly. At the very worst moment the girl came to me.

'*Salut* Narrator. What are you doing here at this time?' I swung around immediately, and hit her clumsily across the side of the head, just once, and her assurance vanished completely. She did not cry out, or run, but stood exactly where I had hit her, her head hanging. She said nothing, just stood there, swaying slightly, with the wind blowing in her hair, her face in deep shadows, like a silent scream.

'I did it for you,' she said finally. 'Can you believe that?'

'You must be joking!'

'You must see yourself, Narrator, if you are ever going to be free.' She walked to the edge of the parapet and leant, looking over it, her hands clasped together.

'Can't you see? We're all base, utterly base, there is nothing at all beautiful in anything.' The sun was now burning down into the ocean, only the last tip of it showing above the sea.

'I wanted to show you that that is the case. I wanted to see it and *feel* it, to feel what it is like. I want you all, everyone to feel that, and know it so they cannot escape it with their little everyday hypocrisies.'

I could not believe anything she was saying, I would not believe it, and all the time was conscious of the noise of the typewriter keys clattering, working on a new manuscript.

'It is all futile anyway. I don't really care now that its over and there's no progress to be made,' she said.

She had become like she had been when I had seen her arguing in the kitchen at Goughly; she had slipped on a new personality, adopted a new character, replacing the others I had known in between. She looked down over the parapet, down into the point where the waves churned up over the river. The cliff was quite vertiginous, the mosque on an over-hang, looking down to where the cliff broke into sharp rocks and boulders at its base.

'It does not matter if you believe me or not. If you do not it means you will survive in this place, and learn to believe nothing that you hear; if you do believe me, only maybe in one tiny part of you, then that is good as well, because it means that no matter what happens to you, you will always be able to trust someone, at least.'

'But why cause all this hurt?'

'You cannot learn if you avoid it. You people, you always avoid it and you do not learn, you have no knowledge of people.'

She drew her coat tightly around her, and shivered. There was no attempt at provocation; her voice was tired and flat.

'How do I know you are not noting everything I say, now, at this moment, to give to Murphy?'

'What if I am? Does it really make any difference? Does it matter if one, two or a million people know what you do? It is all lies anyway. What you do with me can be seen in many ways, and you can take your text as the truth if you wish. In fact I wish you would not, as it may be the truth for only this moment in your life. It is really up to you.'

Her hair blew across her face again and her eyes were fixed on the water where it boiled below. The distant noise of waves could just be heard, and beyond that the noise of the city itself.

'It was Murphy's idea anyway,' she said. 'I only agreed because I hate myself and I cannot bear that, and have to turn it away, to avoid destroying myself. It's all a fantasy about the destruction of you, or that salesman that you believe to be you.'

'That you believe to be me.' I corrected her. 'It is still unacceptable, what you have done.'

'Is it?' I felt her arm around my shoulders and moved away from her. 'Let's go down the cliff,' she said. 'I do not care if you still want me or not. If you do, you can have me. You know that. Most men do.' She began to walk along the parapet, right up to the point where it joined the main wall of the blue mosque, right up against the edge of the cliff, and at that point she disappeared. Up until then I was going to let her go, but I ran after her, curious to discover how she had disappeared, or at least that was part of it. Between the parapet and the wall of the mosque was a gap, no more than 18 inches wide, and she had squeezed through this. I followed her, my face cool against the tiles of the mosque, suddenly sober. We moved along this narrow passage for some yards until we came to some stone steps, where she took off her slippers, and we began to descend by a dusty white path that cut back and forth across the face of the cliff. The mass of rocks above loomed out and over us, as if listening to our every breath, and we began to descend more quickly, the noise of the sea becoming louder. She walked fast, keeping well ahead of me, and did not once look back to see whether I was following or not. Finally we came to a small rock alcove at the foot of the cliffs, where the smell of the sea was strong and refreshing, sharp after the heat of the city in the day. She sat cross-legged.

'Why did you bring me down here?'

She did not reply. Then suddenly from far above came the cry of the mosque, diving and plunging through the sound of the sea, the waves, the evening wind in the rocks. At times it could barely be distinguished, then at times it became clearly a human voice, rising above the waves and fading again beneath the surface of the ocean. She seemed caught in some experience completely her own, quite far away.

'You see why we can only approach each other through lust. You see why that is the easiest way?' She said. Suddenly, I felt completely alone, as if she were not there at all. Then she touched my hand.

'Narrator, will you sleep with me as it was intended?'

'Without Murphy?'

'No Murphy,' she said, and I moved towards her. Each time I made an advance she withdrew from me however, until a point was reached where I could barely see her face, until her whole form seemed to blend, to melt into the evening, and at that point we made love, in the way she had intended.

FRIDAY 10TH OCTOBER

I awoke with a black dread upon me as the events of the previous day re-assembled in my mind. I had breakfast, and the sense of dread was still with me, as if the evening before had been a product merely of what I had drunk, of the sunset and desperation combined. Of course, that was the way it *would* feel in the Hotel Metropole, there at breakfast, with the velvet flunkeys and the silver butter knives and the trolleys full of gateaux. Nevertheless, when I saw the blue hat of the postman through the open doors of the hotel restaurant, I almost expected another damning text. I watched the packages being handed over, while one half of me nagged and raged. How could I have done it? What possible explanation would be acceptable? And yet the experience was different in almost every way from what had happened before. I could not imagine that the writing of the new text would give Murphy any pleasure, not unless he told lies. Maybe that was Maria's intention. I found that my anger with him had now almost entirely faded. She had quite probably had reasons that he was unaware of for colluding with him in that way. In fact, a part of me was happy, that last morning in Tabar. I smiled as I opened the one letter, which had been brought over to me on a silver platter from the reception desk. It was the clearance from Zoboti.

I folded it away carefully in my wallet, taking care not to break the seals as I did so. The document was bulky, in triplicate, and translated into both Arabic and French. Sbiti's name had been crossed off each of the three letter headings, neatly barred out with a ruler and a red pen. It was while I was photocopying the import papers at the corner newsagents for Munton ('you wouldn't believe how many copies you'll need') that a fragment of Sbiti's conversation came back to me: 'The man you asked about . . . the cousin of that scoundrel . . . well, he is back again . . .' It was like a jewel in the desert of the drunken bureaucrat's conversation, and now the sand had been cleared from it by some clarifying, invigorating new breeze. I turned quickly and hailed a taxi to take me to Repair Man's hotel. It was still early, the morning clear and fresh, and the streets around the Hotel Parano seemed attractive, not yet cluttered with the litter of the day's business. The taxi dropped me at the head of the street, and I met him coming out as I entered.

'Repair Man, I've got some good news for you.'

He looked tired and seemed suspicious of me, as if I were a complete stranger to him. He was more untidy than the last time, and looked like a European down and out, in fact he almost seemed to be fading into insignificance. A faint cheesy smell came from him. He was one of those men you would step round on the streets.

'Why did you desert me?' He asked.

'Never mind, I have brought you some good news.'

'You are not an honest man.'

'It is about your cousin.'

'There is never any news. Not news you can believe.'

'Your cousin is back!'

He again looked at me suspiciously, as if I were some kind of agent provocateur trying to undermine his newly established line of non-cooperation.

'I do not believe it,' he said shortly.

'He is back. I have talked with Sbiti.'

'That slug,' he said, and spat in the street.

'Honestly. Look, he is back and I have talked to Sbiti. Sbiti himself has been replaced. He says your cousin is back; thinner, more thoughtful, in his old office.'

Slowly, a smile came across his face, yet in such a way that made clear he would not admit my contribution to it.

'You are sure?'

'Of course I'm sure. Why don't you go there now?'

'My friend, if this is true, it is great news!' He seemed gradually reactivated, to gradually come alive, his cunning, hang-dog, broken expression fading almost as we talked. Then he shook my hand, with due gravity and seriousness, clapped me on the back, smiled a huge smile, before his eyes fixed on the corner of the street where the taxis were, as if calculating how fast he could run to get there.

'My friend. I'm sorry, I mean you understand how urgent business can be . . . I will see you . . . later . . .'

He broke away, and began to run, as fast as a man of his size could do, towards the red taxis. Half way there he turned and came back.

'My friend, one last favour. Can you lend me the money for the taxi?' I gave him a few coins.

'And the hotel. I am sorry, but it is a great anxiety.' Then he smiled again and said: 'No, I must not impose. It is my cousin. He is the one who must pay. Maybe you can come to the tennis club tonight, we can drink?'

'I travel to Goughly tonight, I'm afraid,' I said.

'Oh well. I see you in my new shop. This time it will be motorcycles. Narrator, it is something I have always wanted. You have seen the Jerada photograph?'

'And what about all this philosophy of yours?'

'My friend, I see you, I don't forget you. Philosophy? Philosophy is for the bad times,' and with that he was gone. I could hear his voice coming back faintly from the taxi stand: '6 Dirhams, why that is a presposterous price. The ministry is a matter of a few hundred yards only . . .'

There were no further messages at my hotel that night, and I took the evening train back to Goughly, arriving the following morning. I passed the ruins of Repair Man's shop, and walked up past the plane trees, now fading as autumn approached. I climbed the stairs to our flat. Now that I could hear Murphy's typewriter, I knew I did not want any confrontation. The machine was rattling away, in long rhythmic bursts, as if he were underlining great rambling sentences in some new opus. I had not really expected to find him there, maybe had expected to find only a few scattered clues as to his relationship with Maria: a couple of letters, some washing.

I pushed open the door to the flat and walked over to his room, from where the sound of typing was coming. I entered and found him there, with a towel around his head in the form of a turban, and a pair of dark glasses perched ludicrously on the end of his nose. HE COULD NOT HAVE DONE IT. This thought suddenly came to me with tremendous force. Even as he stood up, saying how great it was to see me, I could see what it was he had been typing. On the page a line of letters, 'nnnnnnnnnggggggg!' There was no way he could have collaborated or produced the manuscripts which I had read.

'It's great, isn't it?' he said, showing me an entire page covered with closely typed and meticulous animal noises.

'Its just got to be the new art form. Just got to be, Narrator, hasn't it?'

I asked him. if he had seen Maria since I left Goughly.

'Maria? Maria? Oh yes, Maria. No, for God's sake Narrator, she's a total nut!'

When I opened my mail there was a note from my bank manager, who was seriously concerned about some letters I had written him in August, during Ramadan. He concluded, saying he could find no trace of the firm I claimed to work for, and had received a report that Société Herzog was in liquidation. The legal department had been informed. Also in the mail there was a postalgram from Tabar, which must have travelled up in the same overnight train as I had taken. It was from Munton and said:

I AM MOST UNHAPPY ABOUT THIS PUMP-HOUSE DEAL OF YOURS. ZOBOTI CHOPPED. NEW MAN SHAKY AND MOSTLY INVISIBLE. SEE YOU EARLIEST. MUNTON.

I put down the postalgram and began to laugh, slowly at first, then louder, until Murphy shouted at me to be quiet; but I really only stopped when I began to hear the secret footsteps of my own loneliness echoing in my head. The window of my room was open, the curtains blowing in. Outside, the sun shone, as it always did.

Dedalus Retro

In its forty-year history Dedalus has produced many titles which enjoyed considerable success or played an important part in the Dedalus story but have disappeared from view. Dedalus Retro aims to republish these titles and find a new audience for them. We begin with 3 novels from the 1980s.

From 1985
Dante Alighieri's Publishing Company – Eric Lane

From 1987
Cry Baby – Ros Franey

From 1989
Mr Narrator – Pat Gray

Dante Alighieri's Publishing Company – Eric Lane

The entry in Dante Alighieri's diary for April 22nd 1980 reads:

What do publishers do, who do not do their own repping, distribution, publicity and writing? I can't help wondering? For instance, if it is a bit quiet on the sales and distribution front, I turn my attention to the publicity and Mediaville. Then there are the accounts' statements to be sent out. When I have some spare time in the evening or on the tube, I write my diary. It is a full and satisfying life.

Read on and be enthralled by the Dead Loss Success Story which has more than a passing resemblance to the early days of Dedalus.

'The greatest publishing story ever told.' *The Guardian*

£9.99   ISBN 978 1 915568 17 5   168p   B. Format

Cry Baby – Ros Franey

"Welcome to a moving and compassionate first novel by Ros Franey, *Cry Baby*. The subject is baby-battering. The book is short. The insights are astute. It has the stamp of real talent and augurs well for the future success of a writer who has a genuine feel for her craft."
Peter Tinniswood in *The Times*

"It is a moving book that seriously questions the pressures of motherhood and whether every woman should feel 'naturally' maternal. Like a modern Raskolnikov, Lisa's actions are frenzied, despicable but identifiable-with. Franey writes with a piercing insight into human nature which is astounding for a first novel."
Time Out

"Suspense and foreboding move alongside the chief players in this auspicious novelistic debut by a British writer. Franey deftly engages the reader's emotions as she spins this disturbing tale."
Publishers Weekly

"It is fortunate for those perpetrators of child abuse that a novelist has at last managed to highlight their trauma in an imaginative and sympathetic light. The cold, stark and unpleasant facts of child abuse usually come to us from newspapers and the real skill of *Cry Baby* is the way the novel explains all the complications which force a person into abusing their own child."
Social Work Today

£9.99   ISBN 978 1 915568 00 7   224p   B. Format

The Cat – Pat Gray

'Gray's reworking of the Animal Farm concept brings in a post–Thatcherite twist. Having peacefully co-existed with his friends Mouse and Rat (the latter carries a briefcase and wears Italian suits), the Cat's owners suddenly leave him to fend for himself. He then has to fall back on feline instincts, placating the furry packed lunches which surround him with promises of consumer goods and burrow ownership. A stylish and witty parable.'
Scotland on Sunday

'Left in an empty house, the Cat – previously pampered with canned food and his owners' affection – learns to hunt again, much to the alarm of the intellectual Mouse and the proletarian, politically aware Rat. As Cat makes inroads into the garden (renting property to voles, for example, and thus discouraging their allegiance with those who would topple him), Mouse and Rat try to stave off the Cat's despotic rise. They discover the Cat's vulnerable area: he hungers not only for the deference of the various rodents he has cowed but also for the affection of humans that he once knew. Gray's satire thus at first seems to target the amorality of the ruling classes, only to turn its attention more squarely to capitalism – the hollow repast that never satisfies, the empty acquisition of material goods.'
Publishers Weekly

£8.99   ISBN 978 1 910213 36 0   124p   B. Format

The Political Map of the Heart – Pat Gray

'Absolutely wonderful! There's a strange tension about it, almost like a melodrama. Beautiful, the way it links the history of Ireland with the troubles in the family. I loved it.'
Lynn Barber in *The Sunday Times*

'This convincing and evocative novel may lack the terrors of involvement and love across the sectarian divide, none the less, it explores the universal confusions and complexities of adolescence from an original perspective.'
C.L. Dallat in *The Times Literary Supplement*

'Pat's teenage romance with the lovely Elaine is tenderly related, their innocent relationship at odds with violence around them. With understated compassion, Gray shows a family torn apart and a love tainted by political divisions. His novel is blissfully free of sentimentality and endless rain that plagues so much Irish fiction.'
Lisa Allardice in *The Independent on Sunday*

£7.99   ISBN 978 1 873982 54 9   196p   B. Format

Dirty Old Tricks — Pat Gray

'Just Read: *Dirty Old Tricks* by Pat Gray. A thriller set in the Northern Irish Troubles. In 1975, in Belfast, finding a murdered schoolgirl counts as "almost normal" in the midst of the civil war going on for a cynical Detective (in the best tradition of Raymond Chandler): "The radio burbled police small talk in the lull of a day when the bad men slept and the honest folk tried to begin their daily business."'
James Doyle in *Book Munch*

'Belfast in 1975 provides a gloomy backdrop for this murder mystery, which opens with RUC officer Michael McCann lying awake, half-expecting to be kidnapped and killed, setting the tone for the discovery of 15-year-old Protestant schoolgirl Elizabeth McCabe, murdered and dumped in a Catholic area. It's a grim enough crime as it is, but the constant presence of armoured cars and automatic weapons adds a further layer of bleakness to the oppressive mood. Even the routine business of door-to-door enquiries becomes a military operation with the potential to escalate into violence. McCann has to consider the possibility that the paramilitaries have sunk low enough to sanction tit-for-tat schoolgirl murders, and it's "not easy to detect clues, in a hard country where men never cried". Creepily compelling, Gray's fourth novel probes deeply into darkness, weaving an atmosphere of tension and distrust that permeates every part of McCann's investigation, including his relationships with colleagues. It's masterfully done, but chilling and hard-hitting stuff.'
Alastair Mabbott in *The Herald*

£9.99   ISBN 978 1 912868 26 1   270p   B. Format

The Redemption Cut – Pat Gray

Belfast, 1976. The city is rife with rackets. Paramilitary gangs, the British Army, Police and Intelligence struggle for control. Will McCann be able to redeem himself by solving the case that haunts him? Will those above him allow him to do so? Pat Gray's second Inspector McCann mystery goes to the heart of the moral darkness that was Ulster's troubles. It is a worthy sequel to *Dirty Old Tricks*.

'Gray tells a very enjoyable story and shows up the entrenched attitudes, the bad behaviour on all sides (*you go climbing up on the moral high ground because there's none of that left says one criminal* to McCann and, when asked *Aren't people meant to be innocent until proven guilty?*, he responds *Not here they're not. It's safer to assume everyone is up to something till you've proof of the opposite.*) Fortunately, McCann has more or less been proved wrong.'
John Alvey in *The Modern Novel*

£9.99   **ISBN 978 1 912868 66 7**   270p   **B. Format**

The Limits of Vision — Robert Irwin

'Very funny: it sparkles with brilliance and has a truly superb ending. I confidently predict that there will never be a better novel about housework.'
The Fantasy Review

'If a world can be seen in a grain of sand, then surely phobia can be found in a handful of dust, or so contends obsessed British housewife Marcia, as she does endless battle with dandruff, the carapaces of roaches, grease, rust, grit, the whole panoply of household detritus. Terrorized by the imminent arrival of her coffee-morning ladies, she vacuums the carpet, only to be bested by the spirit Mucor, whose Latin name embodies all elements of slime and grime and who tries to entice her into the kingdom of filth over which he rules. To avoid him she enters the dazzling cleanliness of the Pieter de Hooch canvas hanging on her wall, invoking de Hooch and a raft of other geniuses – Darwin, Teilhard de Chardin, Leonardo, Blake, Dostoyevski, even Jesus to assist her. The coffee-morning ladies arrive; she half-listens to their prattle while impatiently waiting for them to leave so she can attack the dishes they have dirtied. Soon her husband, whom she suspects of having an affair with one of the ladies, will come home; how can she defeat Mucor before that moment? The solution is in perfect harmony with this astonishing work of imagination and erudition.'
Publishers Weekly

£8.99   ISBN 978 1 912868 57 5   120p   B. Format

The Mysteries of Algiers – Robert Irwin

'Entertaining and very nasty, this calculatedly intellectual comedy succeeds well as an unheroic quest starring Philippe, an interesting monster of disarming modesty.'
The Listener

'Robert Irwin's third novel confirms that, whatever his other main concerns may be, he has thoroughly mastered the art of telling a story. In a plot which snakes and twists, the reader cannot let his concentration drop for a moment. At times the death-defying narrow escapes are firmly in the tradition of James Bond ... as well as being a rattling good yarn, this is a study of moral bankruptcy of those who pursue abstractions through violence ...very successful.'
The Times Literary Supplement

'What separates Irwin's story from the usual spy thrillers is not only his wit and satire but also his verbal pyrotechnics.'
The Washington Post

£6.99   ISBN 978 1 873982 60 0   203p   B. Format

The Revenants — Geoffrey Farrington

'Jaded horror fans who might dismiss British author
Farrington's 1983 cult book as just another vampire
novel would do well to take a second look now that
it's making its American debut. As Kim Newman notes
in his introduction, the tale draws its inspiration from
pre-Dracula vampire fiction and as such its Byronic
hero, John LePerrowne, a member of the Cornish
nobility, experiences what it's like to become a
"revenant" in ways that readers will find refreshingly
novel. Horrified by the excesses of his fellow revenants,
to whom the rest of humanity are naught but cattle
and playthings, LePerrowne seeks solace in the view
that he is, like all predators, merely a part of Nature,
but his exemption from death, to which all things in
Nature are subject, ultimately denies him even that
balm. Instead, he comes to realize that he and his kind
are forever alienated from other life, even from each
other. This is no escapist power-fantasy but rather a
Gothic *bildungsroman* that draws its strength from the
hero's tragic struggle to retain his humanity. It should
appeal greatly not only to devotees of the genre but to
anyone interested in what makes us human.'
Publishers Weekly

'Far superior to most of Anne Rice's empurpled
Gothicism, and, quite possibly, the best vampire novel
since *Dracula*.'
Starred review in *Kirkus*

£7.99   ISBN 978 1 903517 04 8 252p   **B. Format**